P9-BJR-069

"Full-length Comedy"

BEL KAUFMAN'S

Up the Down Staircase

DRAMATIZED BY

CHRISTOPHER SERGEL

THE DRAMATIC PUBLISHING COMPANY

UP THE DOWN STAIRCASE

A Full-Length Comedy

For Twelve Men and Eighteen Women

CHARACTERS

DR. MAXWELL CLARKE.... *High School principal*

SYLVIA BARRETT
BEATRICE SCHACHTER   .... *members of the faculty*
PAUL BARRINGER

J.J. MC HABE
ELLA FRIEDENBERG
FRANCES EGAN   .....*members of the school staff*
CHARLOTTE WOLF
SAMUEL BESTER
SADIE FINCH

LOU MARTIN
LENNIE NEUMARK
CAROLE BLANCA
ALICE BLAKE
VIVIAN PAINE
RUSTY O'BRIEN
LINDA ROSEN
JOSE RODRIGUEZ   ....*students in Room 304*
CARRIE BLAINE
HARRY KAGAN
JILL NORRIS
RACHEL GORDON
ELIZABETH ELLIS
CHARLES ARRONS
EDWARD WILLIAMS
JOE FERONE

HELEN ARBUZZI
FRANCINE GARDNER   ....*other students*
KATHERINE WOLZOW

ELLEN......................... *Sylvia's friend*

PLACE: Calvin Coolidge High School, New York City.
TIME: The present.

"And gladly wolde he lerne,
and gladly teche."

Chaucer's
Clerke of Oxenford

ACT ONE

SCENE: The stage is divided into several sections
which provide several playing areas. The set
stands throughout the play. There is no need
for shifting scenery and accordingly the play can
move quickly without technical complications or
delays.

While it's easier to understand the set from the
diagram, a description follows:

There is a divider or wall-section coming from
the back part of the stage toward the front.   It
is about one-quarter of the way in from the left
and it has a door in it or at least an opening that
can suggest a door.

Between the divider and the right side of the
stage is the main playing area, Classroom 304
of Calvin Coolidge High School. At R are a desk
and chair for the teacher; and URC, facing the
audience, is her blackboard. The remainder of
this area is taken up by student desk-chairs, or
small chairs with desks. There should be twelve
--four fewer than the number of students, the
point being to suggest an overcrowded classroom.

The final feature of this set is one that makes
the fast pace of the play possible, and it adds

5

both fun and excitement to the show. Then, too, it offers an opportunity for the director and cast to use their own imagination in arranging this part of the set. Basically it's a raised platform running across from R to L at the back of the stage. The front of this platform has a series of cut-outs of various sizes and arrangements behind which actors can remain concealed from the audience, and then appear by raising their heads or standing up. (This part of the set can be made even more interesting by having some small doorways which can be swung open by the actor behind, the line delivered, and the door closed. There can also be holes in the cut-outs large enough for an actor to put his head through.)

The cut-outs at the far R and far L sides of the raised platform will later be labeled "Suggestion Box." They are at the two sides to make it easy for a number of actors to get to them easily for a series of quick "suggestions." If there is room enough backstage, there can also be access to the platform by steps directly behind it.

The fronts of the cut-outs may be decorated as desired by the cast and the director. Probably bright colors should be used and there may be a number of things written on them such as "Hi, Teach!" - "Let it be a challenge" - "Please Do Not Erase" - "A for Effort" and so forth as desired.

AT RISE OF CURTAIN: Light comes up with its emphasis on the classroom section of the stage.

SYLVIA BARRETT, an attractive and sensitive

young teacher about to teach her first class, comes on L and enters the classroom. She's carrying a load of material, but at the moment it seems light, for she's so happy to be here. She crosses to the desk, puts down her load, and then looks about, a bit uncertain, but also eager and optimistic.

During the above, DR. MAXWELL CLARKE, the principal of Calvin Coolidge High, stands up from behind the center cut-out on the upper level. His head and shoulders should be visible and perhaps he picks up a hand microphone, suggesting that he's using a P. A. system-- though an actual P. A. system should not be used.

SYLVIA pays only casual attention to DR. CLARKE's speech, as she arranges her materials on the desk.

DR. CLARKE (speaking in an "official" tone).　At- tention, please. This is your principal, Dr. Maxwell Clarke. I wish to take this opportunity on the first morning of the first day of school to extend a warm welcome to all faculty　and staff, and the sincere hope that you have re- turned from a healthful and fruitful　summer vacation with renewed vim and vigor ready to gird your loins and tackle the many important and vital tasks that lie ahead--undaunted. Thank you for your help and cooperation in the past and future.

(As he's talking, BEATRICE SCHACHTER, another attractive　but older and more　experienced teacher, comes in L.)

BEA (nodding toward sound). The same message
    every September. I'm Bea Schachter----
    (Points up.) I have room 508.

SYLVIA. Sylvia Barrett. (Nods toward sound.)
    First time for me.

BEA. Our Dr. Clarke always gives us his pearls
    in pairs--aims and goals, guide and inspire,
    help and encourage, new horizons and broader
    vistas.

SYLVIA (excited; confiding). I'm about to teach my
    first class.

BEA. First ever? (SYLVIA nods.) You're pre-
    pared?

SYLVIA (diffidently). I thought I might begin with
    First Impressions: importance of appearance,
    manners, speech--on which I'll build a case
    for good diction, correct usage, fluent self-
    expression. From there it's just a step----

BEA (a smiling interruption). You're sure you've
    come to the right school?

SYLVIA (puzzled). Calvin Coolidge. Room 304.

BEA (concerned). When I said prepared----

SYLVIA (quickly). I majored in Middle English
    literature. Two courses in Philosophy of
    Education. My master's thesis was on Chaucer.

BEA (not letting herself laugh; cheerfully). Well,
    good luck, Sylvia. If you need help, just
    holler. (Points.) I'm right up there. (She's
    starting off L.)

SYLVIA. Thanks, but----

BEA (has paused at door L). Better you'd studied
    karate!

(SYLVIA looks after her a bit concerned before de-
    ciding it was a joke. She smiles and crosses to
    the blackboard. She picks up a piece of chalk
    and takes a breath. This is a lovely moment in

her life and in a bold hand she writes on the blackboard, "Miss Barrett." As she finishes, STUDENTS start pouring in through the classroom door L. Their individual characteristics, described in "Notes on Characters and Costumes," will become more evident later. At the moment they're a confused mass, coming into their first class on the first day of school. They're noisy, exuberant, tending to talk over each other, asking questions without waiting for the reply. It's important to remember, however, that in addition to first-day excitement, there's also a strong element of testing the new teacher.)

LOU MARTIN (calling cheerfully as he comes in). Hi, teach.

LENNIE NEUMARK. Looka her! She's a <u>teacher</u>?

CAROLE BLANCA. Is this room 304? Are you Mr. Barringer?

SYLVIA. No, I'm Miss Barrett.

ALICE BLAKE. I'm supposed to have Mr. Barringer.

VIVIAN PAINE. You the teacher? You so young.

LENNIE. She's cute! Hey, teach, can I be in your class?

SYLVIA. Please don't block the doorway. Please come in.

CAROLE. Good afternoon, Miss Barnet.

SYLVIA. Miss Barrett. My name is on the blackboard. Good morning.

RUSTY O'BRIEN. Oh, no! A <u>dame</u> for home room?

LOU MARTIN. You want I should slug him, teach?

LINDA ROSEN. Is this home room period?

SYLVIA. Yes. Sit down, please.

LINDA. I'm not sure I belong here.

(JOSE RODRIGUEZ comes in shyly and edges over

to the far corner.)

CARRIE BLAINE. We gonna have you all term? Are you a regular or a sub?

HARRY KAGAN (pompously). There's an insufficiency of chairs!

SYLVIA. Take any seat at all.

JILL NORRIS. Is this room 309?

LOU. Someone swiped the pass. Can I have a pass? (Dying of thirst.) I gotta get a drink of water!

RACHEL GORDON. What's your name?

SYLVIA. My name is on the board.

RACHEL. I can't read your writing.

LOU (in mock agony). I'm dying!

LENNIE. Don't believe him, teach. He ain't dying.

HARRY. Stop your inconsideration of the teacher, you bums.

RUSTY. Can we sit on the radiator? That's what we did last term.

LENNIE. Pipe down, you morons. The teacher's trying to say something.

SYLVIA. Please sit down. I'd like to----

ELIZABETH ELLIS. Will you be teaching *avant-garde* creative writing? (A bell rings.)

SYLVIA (about to answer ELIZABETH but interrupted by bell). That bell is your signal to come to order. Will you please----

LENNIE. When do we go home?

CARRIE. The first day of school and he wants to go home already.

LINDA. Maybe this is the wrong room. What room is this?

SYLVIA. This is room 304. My name is on the board. Miss Barrett. I'll have you for home room all term, and I hope to meet some of you in my English classes. Now, someone said that first impressions----

JILL. English! No wonder!

RACHEL. Who needs it?

LINDA (suspiciously). You give homework?

SYLVIA. First impressions, they say, are lasting. What do we base our first----

(Stops as she sees a girl, FRANCINE GARDNER, who approaches her with a slip of paper. FRANCINE is bored, looking about indifferently.)

SYLVIA. Yes?

FRAN. Mr. McHabe wants Ferone right away.

SYLVIA. Whom does he want?

FRAN. Joe Ferone.

SYLVIA. Is Joe Ferone here?

LENNIE. Him? That's a laugh!

RUSTY. He'll show up when he feels like it. (FRAN exits L.)

SYLVIA. I see. Now. We all know that first impressions---- Yes?

(HELEN ARBUZZI is standing in the door L.)

HELEN. Is this 304?

SYLVIA. Yes. You're late.

HELEN. I'm not late, I'm absent. I was absent all last term.

SYLVIA. Please sit down. (Noting lack of chairs.) I mean--stand up. (Points to back of room.)

HELEN. I can't. I'm dropping out. You're supposed to sign my Book Clearance from last term.

SYLVIA. Do you owe any books?

HELEN (handing her paper; impatiently). I'm not on the blacklist. That's a yellow slip. This is a green! (SYLVIA signs, and HELEN exits

L.)

LOU (during above). Isn't the pass back yet?

LENNIE. Don't you ever give up?

SYLVIA. I'm afraid we won't have time for the discussion on first impressions. I'm passing out----

LOU (shouting; mock alarm). Hey, she's passing out! Give her air.

SYLVIA (handing out cards). I'm passing out attendance cards. Print in ink your last name first, your parents' names, your date of birth, my name--it's on the board--and the same upside down. Then I'll make out the seating plan. Any questions? (The following is almost simultaneous.)

RACHEL. In ink or pencil?

RUSTY. I got no ink--can I use a pencil? Who's got a pencil to loan me?

LOU. I don't remember when I was born.

LENNIE. Don't mind him--he's a comic.

JILL. Print or write?

CARRIE. When do we go to lunch?

LOU. I can't write upside down.

LENNIE. Ha-ha. He kills me laughing.

CAROLE. What do you need my address for? My father can't come.

RUSTY. Someone robbed my ball point!

JOSE (shyly). I don't know my address.

SYLVIA. You don't?

JOSE (with difficulty). We're moving.

SYLVIA. Where are you moving?

JOSE. I don't know where.

SYLVIA. Where do you live?

JOSE. I don't live no place.

SYLVIA (automatically). Any place.

JILL (hand raised). Teach--there's chewing gum on my seat!

RACHEL. First name last or last name first?

LOU. I <u>gotta</u> have a pass to the Men's Room. I
    know my rights. This is a democracy, ain't
    it?

SYLVIA. <u>Isn't.</u> (To VIVIAN, in back.) What's
    your trouble?

VIVIAN. There's broken glass back here--from
    the window.

SYLVIA. Don't touch the broken window. It should
    be reported to the custodian. Does anyone----

LENNIE (jumping up). Me. I'll go. That's Mr.
    Grayson--he's in the basement.

SYLVIA. Tell him it's urgent.

(As LENNIE goes out, another boy, CHARLES
    ARRONS, hurries in.) bump into lennie

SYLVIA. Who are you?

talk to
next to
chair

CHARLES. Sorry I'm late. I was in detention.

SYLVIA. In what?

CHARLES. The Late Room. Where they make you
    sit to make up your lateness--when you come
    late. —Steal chair

SYLVIA. Fill out your card, please.

CAROLE. For parents' names, can I use my aunt?

SYLVIA. Put down your mother's name.

CAROLE. I've got no mother.

SYLVIA. Do the best you can.

(FRAN has come back in L.)

SYLVIA (to FRAN). What is it this time?

FRAN (crossing to hand a piece of paper to SYLVIA).
    Mr. McHabe said you're to read this to your
    class.

SYLVIA. May I have your attention, please. There's
    been a change in today's assembly schedule.

Listen carefully. (Getting a bit confused herself as she reads.) "Please ignore previous
instructions in circular 3, paragraphs 5 and
6, and follow the following: (Clears throat.)
"This morning there will be a long home room
period extending into the first half of the second period. All X2 sections are to report to
assembly the second half of the second period.
First-period classes will begin the fourth period. Second period classes will begin the
fifth period. Third period classes will begin
in the sixth, and so on, subject classes being
shortened to twenty-three minutes, except
lunch--(Takes a quick breath.)"--which will
be normal."

Start throwing

LOU. I didn't hear. What did you say?
RACHEL. What's today's date?
HARRY. It's September, stupid.
JILL. This is a long home room.
SYLVIA. Please. I'm not finished. (Reading.)
    "Tomorrow all Y2 sections will follow today's
    program for X2 sections, while all X2 sections
    will follow today's program for Y2 sections."

(FRAN takes announcement and hurries out, as an-
    other girl, KATHERINE WOLZOW. comes in.
    Her manner is impatient.)

CARRIE (whispering). Where do we go?
VIVIAN. What period is this? (LOU and CHARLES
    are tossing the eraser back and forth.)
SYLVIA. The two boys in the back--stop throwing
    the board eraser. Please come to order.
KATHERINE. Excuse me. Miss Friedenberg--
    from Guidance--she wants Joe Ferone right
    away.
SYLVIA. He isn't here. (KATHERINE exits.) Will

walk back to talk

you pass your attendance cards down, please,
   while I----
VIVIAN. I didn't start yet. I'm waiting for the pen.
RACHEL (to SYLVIA). How do you spell your
   name?
LOU. Hey, he threw the eraser out the window!
SYLVIA. Will you please----

(EDWARD WILLIAMS is entering L. He is black,
   sullen, suspicious, not without cause.)

EDWARD (crossing with papers). Here's my ad-
   mit. He says I was loitering.
SYLVIA. Who?
EDWARD. McHabe.
SYLVIA. Mr. McHabe.
EDWARD (leaning against wall). Either way.
SYLVIA. Class--please finish your cards while I
   call the roll.

(PAUL BARRINGER, a tall and handsome teacher,
   is entering L.)

EDWARD. I never got no card.
PAUL (almost automatically). Any card.
SYLVIA (at the same time). Any card. (She looks
   at PAUL, startled, inquiring.) You are----?
PAUL. Your fellow teacher, Paul Barringer. I
   teach English in 309. (Dropping his voice.)
   Sorry to interrupt, but could I borrow your
   board eraser?
SYLVIA. Yes--no. I'm afraid it's gone.
ALICE (rising; the beginning of a crush). I could
   go get one for you, Mr. Barringer.
PAUL (going). Never mind. (Smiles to SYLVIA.)
   Anyway, we've got something in common.
SYLVIA (blankly). What's that?

PAUL (as he goes off L). No erasers.

SYLVIA (to ALICE). Please, sit down. (To the
    class.) I must take attendance. If I mispro-
    nounce your name, please correct me. (Read-
    ing from Roll Book.) Arbuzzi, Helen.

HARRY. She's dropping out.

                (LENNIE hurries back in L.)

SYLVIA. Oh, yes.

LENNIE. The custodian says there's no one down
    there.

SYLVIA (this is too much). How can he say that
    when he's down there?

LENNIE (shrugging). That's what he says. Any
    answer?

SYLVIA. No answer! (Grips Roll Book again.)
    Blake, Alice?

ALICE (still looking after Paul). I'm present, Miss
    Barrett.

SYLVIA (smiling). You're sure?

ALICE (turning front; embarrassed). Oh, yes.
    Present.

SYLVIA. Blanca, Carmelita?

CAROLE. Carole. I changed my name.

SYLVIA. Blanca, Carole?

CAROLE (enjoying her new name; with a huge
    smile). Here.

                (KATHERINE is back at the door L.)

SYLVIA. Borden . . . (Seeing KATHERINE.) Yes?

KATHERINE. Miss Friedenberg wants the Service
    Credit Cards from last term.

SYLVIA. I'm in the middle of----

KATHERINE. She needs them right away.

SYLVIA. I wasn't here last term.

KATHERINE (going right on with a list). Second,
    the office wants to know are the transportation
    cards ready. (Putting paper on desk.) Third,
    fill this out immediately.
SYLVIA. Not so fast. The what cards ?
KATHERINE. Transportation. Bus and subway.
SYLVIA. I haven't even taken attendance. (Anx-
    iously to LENNIE at the back, who has crowded
    onto seat with another boy.) Please don't tilt
    that chair--boy in the back--I'm talking to you.
    (He falls over.)
LENNIE (scrambling up). So I fell. Big deal!
SYLVIA. Are you hurt?
LENNIE. Naw, just my head.
KATHERINE. You better make out an accident re-
    port, three copies, and send him to the nurse.
LOU. The nurse ain't even allowed to give out
    aspirins. Only tea.
LENNIE. You call this a chair?
HARRY (ominous). He could sue the whole Board
    of Education.
SYLVIA. You'd better go to the nurse. (LENNIE
    starts off L. After him.) And ask her for the
    accident report blanks. (To KATHERINE, who
    still stands there impatiently.) Is there some-
    thing else?
KATHERINE (handing her paper). You're supposed
    to read this to your class. It's from the liberry.
SYLVIA (correcting, automatically). Library.
    Class, attention, please. (Reading.) "The
    school library is your library. All students
    are encouraged to use it at all times. How-
    ever--(Takes quick breath.)"--the library will
    be closed to students until further notice to en-
    able teachers to use it as a workroom for their
    PRC entries."
KATHERINE (as she hurries out). I've got eleven

more messages.

SYLVIA (to class). We'll get back to attendance.

(FRAN enters L.)

SYLVIA. We won't get back to attendance. What is it?

FRAN (bored). New change in assembly program. Your class goes to different rows. X2 schedule rows.

SYLVIA. I see.

FRAN (handing paper, lackadaisically). And this is urgent. From Mr. McHabe.

SYLVIA (reading). "To all teachers. A blue Pontiac parked in front of the school has been over-turned. If the following license is yours----" (Hands it back.) Tell Mr. McHabe I don't drive. Now, class----

(LENNIE is coming back in L.)

LENNIE (as he comes). The nurse says she's all out of accident reports, but she wants the missing dentals.

SYLVIA. Missing dentals? We'll get to that later. (Determined.) I'm going to finish the attendance, and then----(There's a loud bell and the students are jumping up simultaneously, banging desks, etc.) leave papers

RUSTY. Hurray!

LOU. Saved by the bell!

SYLVIA. Just a minute. The bell's much too early. It may be a mistake. We have so much to--please remain in your----

LENNIE (speaking almost simultaneously). That's the bell. You heard it.

HARRY. All the teachers are letting them out.

SYLVIA. But we haven't even finished the . . .

RACHEL. When the bell rings, we're supposed to go!

LINDA. Where do we go, assembly? (They're pouring off L.)

SYLVIA. Please sit down. I'd like to--We haven't----(To ALICE and FRAN.) It looks as if we're the only ones left. You're Alice.

ALICE. Alice Blake. I want you to know how much I enjoyed your lesson.

SYLVIA. Thank you, but it wasn't really----(To FRAN.) There's more?

FRAN (nodding, bored). Just one--you're supposed to announce this to your class--right away.

SYLVIA (reading aloud). "Please disregard the bell. Students are to remain in their home-rooms until the next bell." (Hands it back to FRAN.) Thanks.

FRAN (contrite). Maybe I should've given you this one first.

SYLVIA (after her, as she goes, ruefully). Maybe. (As FRAN exits, SYLVIA is alone. She looks about, a wry smile on her face. She is amused at her earlier naivete. Mocking herself.) And I thought I might begin with the importance of first impressions. (Shakes head to clear it, crosses to sit behind her desk, where she's picking up various papers of different colors and sizes.) Program cards, requisition slips, transportation cards, service credit cards---- (Picks up another paper; puzzled as she reads.) "In the two columns labeled male and female indicate the number of students in your homeroom section born between the following dates----"

(JOE FERONE, a hostile young man, has ambled in L and now stands menacing over her desk.)

JOE (rocking on his heels). You Barrett?

SYLVIA (as he tosses slip on her desk). What's this?

JOE (insolently). Late pass.

SYLVIA (speaking firmly but in a low voice). That's no way to hand it to me.

JOE. My aim is bad.

SYLVIA (her voice rising a little in spite of herself). There's no need for insolence. Please take that toothpick out of your mouth when you talk to me. And take your hands out of your pockets.

JOE. Which first?

SYLVIA. What's your name?

JOE. You gonna report me?

SYLVIA. What's your name?

JOE. You gonna give me a zero?

SYLVIA. I've had just about----(Standing up. Demanding.) What's your name?

JOE. Joe.

SYLVIA. Joe what?

JOE. Ferone. You gonna send a letter home? Take away my lollipop? Lecture me? Spank me?

SYLVIA. All I asked----

JOE (starting back for door). Yeah. All you asked.

SYLVIA. I don't allow anyone to talk to me like that. (The bell rings.)

JOE (as he goes). So you're lucky--you're a teacher.

SYLVIA (left alone; bitterly). So I'm lucky. (She looks up and calls softly.) Hello--Room 508-- Bea Schachter. You said--just holler. (Half humorous, half serious.) Bea--help!

(BEA appears above one of the low panels on the upper level.)

BEA. Having fun?

SYLVIA. I'm having problems. I don't think I even
    understand the language. A student called me
    "Hi, teach!"

BEA (cheerfully). Maybe he liked you. Why not
    answer "Hi, pupe"?

SYLVIA. I don't think I could ever bring off "Hi,
    pupe." And the paperwork! I'm buried beneath
    an avalanche!

BEA. That I can clarify. "Let it be a challenge to
    you" means you're stuck with it. "Keep on file
    in numerical order" means throw in waste-
    basket. "Interpersonal relationships" is a
    fight between kids. "Ancillary civic agencies
    for supportive discipline" means call the cops.
    "Literature based on child's reading level and
    experiential background" means that's all
    they've got in the book room. "Non academic-
    minded" is a delinquent, and "it has come to
    my attention" means you're in trouble.

SYLVIA (not knowing whether to laugh or to cry).
    That I believe.

BEA. Did you get anything done in homeroom?

SYLVIA. I took attendance--as far as B. A boy
    fell off a chair. And I forgot to have them
    salute the flag--which may be illegal.

BEA. On assembly days, they salute in the audi-
    torium. What's illegal now is Bible reading.

SYLVIA (smiles). How about a short silent prayer?

BEA. Only if the word "prayer" isn't mentioned and
    if you don't move your lips. And remember--
    there's no such think as a Permanent Pass to
    the Water Fountain.

SYLVIA (holding up a paper from her desk). What
    do I do about the P-P-P's?

BEA. Almost sings, doesn't it? That's the Pupil
    Personality Profile, invented by Ella

Friedenberg, Guidance Counselor--who thinks she's Sigmund Freud.

(ELLA FRIEDENBERG is standing up from behind one of the low cut-outs on the upper level.)

BEA. She bases her P-P-P's on such interview questions as "Why do you hate your parents?"

ELLA (aside to BEA). If I don't ask, how do I find out? (Turns front. In brisk lecture tone.) Latent maladjustments may exhibit themselves in socially unacceptable behavior in the classroom. This is a crucial period in the development of the adolescent. Please send all new pupils to me for in-depth coverage. (As she's going. An afterthought.) However, send the disruptive elements to Mr. McHabe. (ELLA is no longer visible.)

SYLVIA. Mr. McHabe again.

BEA. Administrative Assistant. He's very strict. I don't know--maybe he has to be, but try to avoid him. He's in charge of discipline, and supplies. He can't bear to part with a rubber band. Ask him for a pencil and he turns white.

(MC HABE has risen during the above speech from behind another cut-out on the upper level.)

MC HABE (to the front; forcefully). To all Faculty: Diligence, accuracy, and promptness are essential in carrying out all instructions. Teachers with extra time are to report to the office to assist with activities which demand attention. Regarding the requisition of supplies, please anticipate your needs. (Turns toward BEA.) Do not make excessive demands. (Front again. A bit easier.) Any teachers wishing decorative

posters, we have a few left. Block letters,
blue on white: "Knowledge is Power" and
yellow on green: "Truth is Beauty." (Sitting.)
Also brown and tan of Swiss Alps. Slightly
torn but still usable.

(FRANCES EGAN, wearing a white smock, stands
up from behind another cut-out as MC HABE
disappears behind his.)

FRANCES (front). Students delinquent in obtaining
athletic suits are to be alphabetized and re-
ported. (Dropping her voice slightly.) Girls
who wish to be excused from Gym are to be
sent to me with all pertinent data.
BEA (explaining to SYLVIA). Frances Egan. The
school nurse.
FRANCES (emphatically). Please discourage excessive dieting in your home room.

(FRANCES sits as CHARLOTTE WOLF appears at
another point on the upper level.)

CHARLOTTE (grimly). No books are to be removed
from the library until the card catalog is brought
up to date.
SYLVIA (as CHARLOTTE goes). The librarian?
BEA (nodding). Charlotte Wolf.

(SAMUEL BESTER has appeared at the upper level.)

MR. BESTER (slightly pained to have to say this).
Do not encourage students to purchase paper-
back editions of Shakespeare and other authors.
Because of outside pressures we should not ex-
pose them to insufficiently edited or unexpur-
gated texts.)

BEA (as he goes off). Samuel Bester. Chairman
     of the English Department. A brilliant teacher,
     so naturally he's promoted right out of the
     classroom.

          (A MAN leans in from the side.)

MAN. Hello there, teachers. Looking forward to
     the new school year? Easy Term Confidential
     Loan Company can solve your problems.
BEA (as he goes off). At eighteen per cent.

(SADIE FINCH has come on the upper level at the
     other side.)

SADIE (sounding like a mimeograph machine).
     Teachers should function according to instruc-
     tions. This means hand in on time!
BEA. Sadie Finch, School Clerk.
SADIE. Pupils are to report back to their home-
     rooms to be checked off at 2:56. Dismissal
     bell will ring at 3:05 sharp. (Going off.) This,
     however, is uncertain.

          (MC HABE is on again.)

MC HABE. Send legitimate latenesses to the Late-
     ness Coordinator. If excuse is invalid or sus-
     pect, send offenders to me. Please read to
     your students the list of infractions and penal-
     ties to instill in them a sense of civic respon-
     sibility. Post in a prominent place in home-
     room "A student who is late--may fail to grad-
     u-ate." (He goes.)
BEA. Have to leave you now. I'm trying to salvage
     a potential dropout.
SYLVIA (after her). The very first girl I called on

today was dropping----(But BEA has gone. Remembering.) Arbuzzi--Helen.

(HELEN steps in from L on the lower level.)

HELEN (speaking to the front, though talking to SYLVIA). I've got to drop out, Miss Barrett. I've got to work. I'm of age and my income is needed at home.

SYLVIA (also speaking to the front though talking to the girl). Why don't we talk this over, Helen? Perhaps we could find some way to solve----

HELEN (in a hurry to go). Why talk? Most school is a waste anyhow, every period another subject--Algebra, French, Eco, English, one after the other--what good is it?

SYLVIA. If you'd give me a chance to----

HELEN. It's all a jumble and in every class the teacher tells you something different, till you don't know who to believe.

SYLVIA. But before you take this step that's going to affect your whole life, we should at least----

HELEN. Save your breath. (As she exits L.) I'm better off out.

(MC HABE appears on the upper level.)

MC HABE (in an official voice). Miss Barrett.
SYLVIA (startled). Yes?
MC HABE. It has come to my attention that you have neglected to fill out form B22 Accident Report of a fall from a chair incurred by a student in your official class. Such negligence may result in serious consequences.
SYLVIA. But he wasn't hurt. (Earnestly.) Mr. McHabe, my real concern----
MC HABE (interrupting). Before leaving the

building today, please make out Form B22 in
triplicate.

SYLVIA (resigned). Yes, Mr. McHabe.

MC HABE (briefly). Thank you. (Calling to someone else off L as he goes off upper L.) You,
there. Just a minute!

(SYLVIA turns to look at the blackboard where she
sees her boldly written name. As she considers it, PAUL BARRINGER comes in lower
L.)

SYLVIA (amused at herself, addressing the blackboard). I think you were expecting a little too
much, Miss Barrett.

PAUL (pleasantly). Admiring your penmanship?

SYLVIA (looks to him, smiles, then turns back to
the blackboard). Suddenly my name looks un-
familiar to me. I have a strange feeling I
didn't even spell it right.

PAUL (bringing hand from behind his back, with a
gift). For the school teacher who has everything.

SYLVIA (accepting; pleased). A board eraser.
Thank you.

PAUL. McHabe wasn't around, so I took two.

SYLVIA (wryly to blackboard as she erases name).
You'll have to do better, Miss Barrett.

PAUL (smiles as he's going). *Sauve qui peut.*
(Pauses at door L, looks at watch.) I have a
free--oops--unassigned period. I'll be having
coffee in the Teachers' Lounge.

SYLVIA (eagerly). Maybe I'll----(Catches herself;
speaking more casually.) If I can get through
the locker assignments----

PAUL (as he exits L). Then I'll see you.

SYLVIA (looks after him, then turns and calls up in

a hushed voice). Bea! Bea Schachter!

(BEA appears again on the upper level.)

BEA (humorously). I'm with child.

SYLVIA (chuckles). Then quickly--you haven't told
me about Paul Barringer.

BEA (with slight smile and raised eyebrow). The
glamour boy of the English Department. Unpublished writer. Such men are dangerous.
He'll woo you with rhymes. (Going.) You're
on your own.

SYLVIA (hesitating). I see.

(MC HABE, holding JOE FERONE firmly by the
arm, comes on lower L.)

MC HABE. A moment, Miss Barrett--was Joe
Ferone in home room this morning? Did he
stay till the bell?

SYLVIA. He was a little late, but he stayed till the
bell.

MC HABE. You're certain? It's important. (She
compresses her lips, unwilling to answer a
second time. Realizing he has to explain.) A
valuable wallet was stolen from a locker during
home room, and I understand Ferone was seen
loitering in that vicinity just before the bell.

SYLVIA. Then it couldn't have been Joe. He was in
home room.

MC HABE (almost disappointed). I see. Was he
any trouble?

SYLVIA. Trouble?

MC HABE (exasperated). Disruptive? Rude? Any
trouble? (SYLVIA glances at JOE, who is watching her narrowly.)

SYLVIA (deciding). No. No trouble.

MC HABE. If you think it helps to cover for them,
      then you're very much mistaken.
SYLVIA. Unless there's something else, Mr.
      McHabe, I'm going for a cup of coffee. (Taken
      aback, he shakes his head, and SYLVIA walks
      past him and off L. They both look after her
      for an instant. Then JOE reaches down and
      takes McHabe's hand away from his arm.)
JOE. Better luck next time, McHabe.
MC HABE. Mister McHabe.
JOE (smiles as he goes off L). Mister.
MC HABE (after JOE; sure of himself). Every
      year I deal with a lot like you.

(As MC HABE follows JOE off L, FRANCES EGAN
      appears on the upper level.)

FRANCES (concerned). Please ascertain the num-
      ber of students who have not had a hot breakfast
      this morning. Now that winter is approaching
      this is particularly important. Poor nutrition
      is frequently the cause of poor marks.

(JILL NORRIS enters DL carrying copies of the
      school newspaper with which she crosses to R.)

JILL (calling as she crosses from L to R). Calvin
      Coolidge Clarion. Get your copy of the Clarion.
      Don't miss the Halloween issue--just out today.
      Interviews--a message from our principal. (As
      she goes off.) Important advertisements.

(A MAN leans in L.)

MAN. The Corner Coffee Shoppe "Where Friend
      Meets Friend."
                (A WOMAN leans in R.)

WOMAN. Compliments of the Vanity Corset
    Company.

    (DR. CLARKE appears on the upper level.)

DR. CLARKE (pompously). Your education has
    been planned and geared to arm and prepare
    you to function as mature and thinking citi-
    zens. I'm sure you will all prove worthy and
    deserving of our trust and expectations--
    Signed: Dr. Maxwell Clarke, Principal.

(As he sits out of sight, RACHEL GORDON steps
    in L.)

RACHEL. Faculty Flashes from the *Clarion*. The
    teacher the girls would like to be on a desert
    island most with: Mr. Paul (Poet) Barringer.
    The teacher readiest with unselfish helps: Mrs.
    Bea (Mom) Schachter. Most glamorous teach-
    er: Miss Sylvia Barrett. She's only been with
    us since September, but we hope she stays a
    while.

(JILL has come on R during above. RACHEL is
    going off L.)

JILL. As a special service, your *Clarion* has in-
    augurated a lost and found column. (Takes
    breath.) First we'll list--Lost!

    (LOU stands on the upper level.)

LOU. Green plaid jacket, tore lining, broke zipper.
    Urgent need! Signed Lou Martin.

    (LINDA stands next.)

LINDA. Make-up kit, imitation red alligator.
    Linda Rosen.

(ALICE stands next.)

ALICE. Hollywood Horoscope of Stars magazine.
    Reward. Alice Blake.

(EDWARD stands.)

EDWARD. Lost--or stole! My left lens from my
    eyeglasses between here and History. Edward
    Williams, Esquire.
JILL. Now for--Found! (She waits expectantly, but
    there is no response. The still standing students
    look at each other, shake their heads and go off.)
    No founds. (She shrugs.) Students--the *Clarion*
    is the Voice of Your School. Please subscribe.
    (As she exits R.) And solicit ads to keep it
    talking.

(SADIE FINCH has appeared again on the upper
    level.)

SADIE. All teachers, attention. Do not accept
    lateness excuse due to fire on the subway. This
    was checked by Mr. McHabe with the Transit
    Authority. There was no fire on the subway.

(During this, KATHERINE has come on L, bringing
    some papers which she's reading as she crosses
    to Miss Barrett's desk.)

KATHERINE (reading). "Mr. McHabe to Miss
    Barrett. Please note that Joe Ferone has been
    placed on probation. Truant Officer reports no
    such address as the one given. Subject teachers

claim he's been cutting classes. Nurse says
he's on Dental Blacklist." (Puts papers down
on desk as though too hot to handle, but as she
starts away she gives them farewell pat.) Lots
of luck, Joe.

(The lights are dimming quickly as KATHERINE
goes off L, and a spot has come up on a part
of the upper level at ULC. ELLEN, who is
Sylvia's friend, is coming into the spot of
light. She holds an opened letter.)

ELLEN (calling back L as she comes into light).
Watch the baby a minute, please. I've a letter
from my friend Sylvia. We went through college
together. Now she's teaching in New York.
(She turns front, and starts skimming through
the letter.) "A far cry from Graduate School
and Professor Winters' lectures on 'The Psy-
chology of the Adolescent.' I have met the
adolescent face to face. Obviously Professor
Winters had not."

(During this, SYLVIA enters L, then crosses to
another spot of light that comes up at DRC.)

NOTE: *In all these exchanges between SYLVIA
and ELLEN, the actresses playing these roles
should indicate clearly when they are reading
a letter and when they are having direct conversation. This can be done in part by looking
at a letter itself, and then by talking directly
to the other. When conversation goes back into correspondence, the letter should again be
in view.*

ELLEN (smiling as she continues reading). "While

you're strolling through your suburban super-
market with your baby in the cart, or taking a
shower in the middle of third period----"

SYLVIA (picking up with what apparently is in the
letter). I'm automatically erasing the latest
graffiti from the blackboard. Even the building seems hostile--cracked plaster, broken
windows, carved-up desks, gloomy corridors.
I've been here only two months, and already
I'm in a battle I'll probably lose.

ELLEN (addressing her directly). Over the boy
you mentioned in your last letter?

SYLVIA (nodding unhappily). Joe Ferone--insolent,
contemptuous--very bright but flunking every
subject.

ELLEN. Why fight for that one?

SYLVIA (she too is wondering why). I don't know.
Maybe because I sense something in his rebel-
liousness that's like mine--that's against the
same things. Or maybe it's just because he's
been so damaged.

ELLEN. You're not there to fight for them. You're
a teacher.

SYLVIA (ruefully). I keep thinking of Mattie who
was in college with us. Right now she's at
Willowdale Academy holding seminars on James
Joyce under the philosophic maples.

ELLEN. What keeps you from Willowdale? That
other teacher--Paul something?

SYLVIA. Barringer?

ELLEN (eagerly). Tell me about him.

SYLVIA (considering). All I really know--he's
clever, attractive. (Troubled.) But there's
something about him that--eludes.

ELLEN (curious). Eludes?

SYLVIA (trying to sort it out). It's hard to say. For
one thing he waits till the hall traffic subsides

before he leaves his room. I have an impres-
sion he does this to avoid being touched by the
kids. And he seems just passing through here
--marking time teaching till he gets published
and he can leave.

ELLEN. And you and the girl students find this in-
triguing.

SYLVIA (smiling). Devastating. There's a girl in
my class, Alice Blake, who's almost love-sick
over the man.

(ALICE has come up to SYLVIA from R, joining her
in the spot of light.)

ALICE. The thing I really like about him, Miss
Barrett----

SYLVIA (trying to stop her). Please, Alice.

ALICE. He never sits behind the desk. Either he
leans against it, or he sits on top. And have
you noticed--one eyebrow is higher than the
other?

SYLVIA (insisting). Alice--the subject is Homer's
The Odyssey.

ALICE. I know. Also *The Myths and Their Meaning*
But have you ever noticed----

SYLVIA (gently propelling her L). I'm looking forward to your paper.

ALICE (giving up; as she goes off L). Yes, Miss
Barrett.

ELLEN (curiously; to SYLVIA). Well, have you?

SYLVIA. Have I what?

ELLEN. Noticed his eyebrows?

SYLVIA. The one that's higher than the----(Stopping herself. Irked.) What possible difference
does----(Glances L, where she sees someone.)
Sorry. I can't finish now.

ELLEN (reading again, from the letter in her hand).

"I think it's Paul coming. I'll send the rest of this letter tomorrow."

(ELLEN is moving L out of the light, and PAUL is entering L on the lower level and crossing to join SYLVIA in her spot of light.)

PAUL (as he comes; indicating L). What's the matter with Alice Blake?

SYLVIA (defensively). There's <u>nothing</u> the matter with Alice Blake.

PAUL (pleasantly). Don't bite <u>my</u> head off. Especially now, because you're about to be immortalized--I've found a rhyme for Sylvia Barrett.

SYLVIA. Nothing rhymes with Barrett.

PAUL (suavely). Fourteen karat. (As she smiles.) Why did you insist on going home right after dinner last night? I thought we were having a pretty nice time.

SYLVIA (regretfully). Papers to mark.

PAUL. No one can take it that seriously. You were put <u>off by</u> my bad mood. It was the latest rejection slip. The tone is not only polite, but patronizing. Why don't I write of something familiar?

SYLVIA (gently). Well?

PAUL (with disdain). What do they want me to write about? Calvin Coolidge High School?

SYLVIA. At least they couldn't say you're not familiar with----

PAUL (cutting in; irritated). Kids sprawling in classrooms, yawning in assembly, pushing through halls----

SYLVIA. That's the surface, Paul. If you'd get closer----

PAUL. Do <u>you</u> get closer?

SYLVIA. I'm trying, but----(Ruefully.) I haven't

even found what to call them yet--teenagers, youngsters, kids, young adults? Those expressions all seem stilted, inappropriate, even offensive.

PAUL. Let it go at pupil load. (Eagerly.) Sylvia-- I've started on a new novel. This one's going to make it. Let's have a cup of coffee later and I'll tell you about it.

SYLVIA. Sure, Paul.

PAUL. A big subject. (Starting L, off into the darkness.) A nuclear physicist--he's marooned on a peninsula--in Kamchatka.

(As PAUL exits L, ELLEN enters on the raised platform, reading a letter as she comes to ULC.)

ELLEN (continuing out loud with letter). "I looked up Kamchatka. It's at the far eastern end of Russia--opposite Japan." (Addressing SYLVIA directly.) Maybe he knows all about it, sister. Maybe he reached Calvin Coolidge High via the Trans-Siberian railroad.

SYLVIA (smiling). More likely the subway.

ELLEN (curious). Are you reaching the students?

SYLVIA. No--but there was a beautiful moment yesterday. For the first time I was able to excite a class with an idea. I put on the board Browning's "A man's reach should exceed his grasp or what's a heaven for?" (With growing excitement.) And then we were involved--a spirited discussion--aspiration versus reality. (Turning L, as though asking class.) Is it wise to aim higher than one's capacity?

VOICES (from the darkness, L). Yes! No!

SYLVIA (to L). Does it doom one to failure?

VOICES (L; excited). Of course! Don't be stupid!

How ya gonna make progress? What about
ambition? So what? So all ya do, you get
frustrated.
SYLVIA (to L). And hope? What about hope?
VOICES. You've got to be practical. I say you've
    got to have a dream. Hitch your wagon to a
    star. What about--shoemaker stick to your
    last? Miss Barrett--call on me! My turn!
    Call on me! Oh, please--let me talk!

(A light suddenly reveals MR. MC HABE's face,
    just inside doorway L.)

MC HABE (furious). Miss Barrett!

(NOTE: MC HABE can be holding a flashlight
    pointed at his face from below.)

SYLVIA (startled). Yes? Yes, Mr. McHabe?
MC HABE. Can't you keep your class in order?
SYLVIA. They're in order. (Collecting herself.)
    We're in order.
MC HABE. Then what's the meaning of this?
SYLVIA (bewildered). Meaning of what?
MC HABE (she must be an idiot). All this noise?
SYLVIA (gathering force). The noise, Mr. McHabe?
    That's the sound of thinking! (They stare at
    each other for a moment. Then MC HABE takes
    a breath.)
MC HABE (turning slightly as though addressing the
    class). There will be a series of three bells
    rung three times indicating Shelter Drill. (Back
    to SYLVIA.) Loud discussions do not encourage
    the orderly evacuation of the class. (The light
    on him snaps off as he turns to exit L.)
ELLEN (after an instant of consideration). I suppose
    he has his problems, too.

SYLVIA. But keeping order is getting to be the important thing. Enthusiasm is frowned on because it gets noisy. I don't know that I'm
reaching them at all. Maybe other English
teachers are more successful----

ELLEN (smiling as she goes). Let it be a challenge
to you.

SYLVIA. How do other teachers----(ELLEN is
gone. SYLVIA turns.) Class--can you tell me
what you've gotten out of English so far?

(STUDENTS are standing up on the platform. They
speak, one following the other quickly, and
then they go off.)

HARRY. During my many years of frequenting
school, I'm well satisfied with my instruction,
and I hope to achieve further progress in my
chosen program of study with----

LOU (putting hand over his mouth to stop him).
Okay, Harry.

LINDA. What I got out of it is literature and books.
But having boys in class distracts me from my
English. Better luck next time.

CHARLES. I hope this term with you will be good
because you seem to be alive--though it's too
early to tell.

LENNIE. Being you're still new, you should know
I made a bargain with my teachers. If I don't
bother them, they won't bother me.

SYLVIA (calling on him). Edward.

EDWARD (correcting her). Edward Williams,
Esquire. (She nods agreement and he continues.)
All the teachers flunk me because I'm black.
Frankly, I would prefer a teacher freely tell-
ing me I'm no good in English than giving me
dirty looks in the hall.

RUSTY. What I learned in English is to doodle. It's such a boring subject, I spend a lot of time doodling.

LOU. Essays--a lot of gossip. *Ivanhoe* is for the birds. George Eliot stinks, even though he's a lady.

ELIZABETH. A kaleidoscope. A crazy quilt. An ever-shifting pattern. Shapes that come and go, leaving no echo behind. Such is my remembrance of lost and vanished hours of English from whence I arise, all creativity stifled, yet a Phoenix with hope reborn. Will it be different this term? The question, poised on the spear of time, is still unanswered. (Changing tone. Directly to SYLVIA.) I was supposed to be in Mrs. Schachter's Creative Writing class, but because of a conflict, I couldn't get in.

SYLVIA (smiling). Sorry about that. Let me ask a specific question. Why do we study myths? *The Odyssey?*

RACHEL. Because we want to talk like cultured people. At a party how would you like it if someone mentioned a Greek god and you didn't know him? You'd be embarrassed.

EDWARD. What good is integration if I still get hard assignments?

VIVIAN. We study myths to learn what it was like to live in the golden age with all the killings.

JILL. If it wasn't for myths, where would Shakespeare be today?

ALICE. We study myths because they're about love.

CARRIE. To me, the *Odyssey* was just another *Ethan Frome* or *Silas Marner*. Who wants to hear about someone's troubles?

LOU. Everyone has to read them, and it's our turn.

CAROLE. Myths help us gain tolerance for others
    --even if they don't deserve it.
JOSE. We read it because it's a classical.
LENNIE. My opinion is that I hated the *Odyssey*.
    (Confidentially.) Homer is a lousy writer.

(The lights are coming up on the classroom.
    LENNIE, the last student on the platform to
    speak, has stepped down. At the same time,
    JOE FERONE, hands in pockets, comes on
    L. He stands outside the doorway to the
    classroom, facing front.)

JOE (to SYLVIA, but talking front). Why do you
    ask these questions? What are you trying to
    prove? No one in this school gives a damn
    about us, and it's the same at home and in the
    street outside. You probably don't care for
    my language, so give me a zero in vocabulary.
    Anyhow, I'm quitting the end of this term--
    joining the dogs eating dogs in the lousy world
    you're educating us for. But don't worry.
    You'll still find plenty willing to play your game
    of baah baah little lambs, trot in step and get
    your nice clean diplomas--served on dirt.
    Yummy! I trust this answers your question.
SYLVIA (answering, but talking to front). You ex-
    press yourself vividly, Joe. And your meta-
    phors--from dogs to lambs--are apt. I'd give
    you higher marks than you'd give yourself.
    Joe--before you decide to quit, we should talk.
    Can you see me after school today? There's
    so much--I wish I could convey what I----
JOE (mocking). I don't understand them big words,
    and I'm busy after school. Every day. You'll
    have to prove yourself on your own time, teach.
    (The bell rings. JOE turns and comes into the

classroom.)

SYLVIA (regarding him cautiously).   The first time
    you've ever been early.

JOE. I missed the class before this, because of
    McHabe.

SYLVIA. Mr. McHabe.

JOE (tossing paper onto her desk).   He said give
    you this.

SYLVIA (reading).   "Please admit bearer to class.
    He was detained by me for going up the down
    staircase and subsequent insolence. J. J.
    McHabe."

JOE (sarcastically). Think of that!

SYLVIA. Sit down, please. Did you bring your
    homework? (He shakes his head.) Why not?

JOE (as he sits). I didn't do it.

SYLVIA. Why?

JOE. I just didn't.

SYLVIA (strong). Some day you'll have to prove
    yourself, Joe. You have so much you're not
    using. You could----

(The other STUDENTS are coming into the class-
    room.)

JOE (interrupting). I'm supposed to accelerate at
    my own speed. I'm supposed to compete with
    myself. Well, maybe I'm not so hot.

SYLVIA. I happen to know your I.Q. . . . and it's
    pretty hot. (Turning to others.) We have a
    test today, so hurry along, please. And turn in
    your homework. (They are all taking their
    seats.)

RUSTY. Homework? (Indignant.) Someone stole
    my homework!

HARRY (apologetic). It's like this. I fell asleep
    on the subway because I stayed up all night doing

my homework. So when it stopped at my sta-
tion, I ran through the door not to be late--
and left my homework on the subway.

CAROLE. As I was taking down the assignment,
my ball point stopped.

JILL. I had to study French, so I didn't have time
for English.

RACHEL. My brother took my homework instead
of his homework.

VIVIAN. The page was missing from my book.

EDWARD. If a teacher wants to know something,
why doesn't she look it up herself instead of
making we students do it?

JOSE. There's no room, because my uncle moved
in and I have to sleep in the hall and can't use
the kitchen table.

CARRIE. The baby spilled milk all over it.

LINDA (logically). In those hours when I have to
do homework, I can watch TV.

LOU. What homework?

LENNIE. I hate to tell you this--a terrible tragedy.
(A gesture of despair.) My dog went on my
homework!

SYLVIA (laughing as she passes out test papers).
All right, Lennie. That makes it unanimous.
(ALICE slips some papers to her.) Not quite
unanimous. (To ALICE.) Thank you.

CAROLE. Why so many tests, teach?

SYLVIA. I learned your name, Carole. Couldn't
you learn mine?

CAROLE. We see you every day. Why do we hafta
be formal?

HARRY. Because it's protocol--dum dums. Right,
Miss Barrett?

CHARLES. You're a teach. Why not call you Teach?

SYLVIA. Don't open the test booklet till I tell you.

LENNIE. I don't care if I never open it.

LOU (leaning back). Anything you say, teach.

SYLVIA (having noticed; putting a paper face-down on Alice's desk; aside). This doesn't seem to be part of your homework, Alice. (ALICE turns the paper right side up, sees what it is, and gasps with embarrassment.)

ALICE (aside to SYLVIA). You didn't read it?

LINDA (snatching paper). Read what?

CARRIE (snatching it from LINDA). Let me see.

CHARLES (looking over Carrie's shoulder). A big heart with Paul!

CARRIE (reading). "Memorize all poetry Barringer reads."

CAROLE (defending). Hey, leave her alone----

LINDA (snatching paper back). I had it first---- (Reading. Dramatically.) "His voice--the way his eyebrow goes up--how to describe the----" (SYLVIA takes the paper from her.)

SYLVIA. That's enough. (Sharply.) If you want your own privacy respected, respect it in others.

LINDA (giggling). Honest, teach----

SYLVIA (correcting). Miss Barrett. (Hands paper back to ALICE.) Put this away. (Crossing back to her desk.) You're not to open your test booklets till I say "start." (Picking up paper from desk.) Before we start, please pay attention to this directive. (As she reads, the lights gradually dim except for a spot on ALICE, who still stares at the paper SYLVIA gave back to her. SYLVIA reads the directive briskly.) "The fact that Thanksgiving falls when it does this year is causing difficulties in midterm examination schedules. Since there will be no final exams, midterm marks will count as two-thirds of the final mark. Students are to place on the floor all books, notebooks,

and personal possessions. Students may not
leave their seats for any reason whatsoever.
The proctor is to approach them at their seats
to answer questions. (Takes a breath.) "No
questions are to be answered by the proctor.
If a student desires to go to the lavatory, the
proctor will escort the student to the door and
summon the hall proctor who will escort the
student to the lavatory--male teachers will escort boys, female teachers will escort girls.
Students must understand the importance of
high ethical standards. "

(The light has dimmed off through this except for
the spot on ALICE BLAKE, whose mind has
drifted to that which is most important to her.)

ALICE (talking to herself). His voice--the way his
eyebrow goes up--how to describe the emotion
----(As though addressing him; speaking softly but with utter sincerity.) If I could die for
you, Paul--like the Lady of Shalott you read to
us about, floating dead on the river under his
window, and Lancelot never knowing--saying
only "She has a lovely face, the Lady of
Shalott. " In my bed at night I pray to the ceil-
ing--please make him love me or notice me in
class where I sit. Make him take me in his
bold, throbbing embrace! When I look at the
cracks in the ceiling and how ugly everything
is, I think it's unreal, my house and my parents!
(The general light begins coming up again.)
Real life is somewhere else--on moonlit ter-
races--in tropic gardens--foreign cities--dark-
ling woods----(The light is now up.)
SYLVIA (calling for attention). All right, class.
(Looks at watch.) Ready--start. (They open

their booklets, register on the first questions,
and then, almost simultaneously, they all
groan.) Get on with it. (With vast sighs, winc-
ing and indignation they start the test. SYLVIA
gives a little sigh herself, and sits behind her
desk. She notices ALICE and gestures for her
to get on with the test.) You, too, Alice.
(ALICE nods and turns to test.)

(BEA appears on the platform where she regards
the thoughtful SYLVIA.)

BEA (a half-whisper). Sylvia--hi! (As SYLVIA
looks up.) I see you have your test under way,
too. (Curious.) What do you think about while
they take a test?
SYLVIA. I think about----(Stopping herself.) I
should be thinking about this pile of "Due before
3" mimeos.
BEA. Are you onto the official gobbledegook yet?
Can you translate the following: illustrative
material?
SYLVIA. Magazine covers.
BEA (nodding). Enriched curriculum?
SYLVIA. Teaching "who" and "whom."
BEA. Right again. What about--all evaluation of
students should be predicated upon initial goals
and grade level expectations?
SYLVIA. It means--if the boy shows up, pass him.
BEA (approving). You're coming along fast. (JOE
FERONE has raised his hand.)
JOE (demanding). Hey--Barrett!
SYLVIA (aside to BEA). Trouble. (Getting up from
desk.) Yes, Joe?
JOE. I have to be excused.
SYLVIA. We're in the middle of a test. (As others
are looking up.) Please continue.

RUSTY. What's the answer to question four?

CAROLE (suspiciously). I don't think we covered part of this.

SYLVIA. No talking. Please do your best.

JOE (has stood up; sharply). Barrett!

SYLVIA. Finish your test.

JOE. I want to go to the lavatory.

SYLVIA (crossing toward him). Couldn't you wait till after----

JOE (cutting in). No.

BEA (calling a soft warning). Careful, Sylvia.

SYLVIA (to JOE; dropping her voice). You have to be escorted.

JOE. So get an escort.

SYLVIA (to class). Keep your eyes on your work. (Looks out L.) I don't see----(Calling off L.) Proctor! Hall Proctor!

JOE (starting off). I'll be back in a few minutes.

SYLVIA (holds his arm). There's no escort.

JOE (regarding her). So what are ya gonna do? (Their eyes clash. SYLVIA takes her hand away.)

SYLVIA (speaking softly, but with decision). I'm going to trust you. Do I have your word you won't get help or look up answers?

JOE (with mock servility). Sure do, teach.

SYLVIA (still speaking softly; curious). Does showing disrespect make you feel better, Joe? More important? A bigger man? (He glares at her, but has no answer. He turns and goes out L. SYLVIA starts back to her desk.)

LENNIE. Some of these questions!

SYLVIA. Don't waste time. (Sharply.) Just do your paper, Charles.

CHARLES (indignant). I'm not cheating. I'm left-handed.

SYLVIA. Since five minutes ago?

CHARLES. Okay, I'll do it right-handed. Whatever
you say, teach.

SYLVIA (looking up to BEA, who is still watching).
I shouldn't have let him go.

BEA (gently). Probably not. (The class continues
with the test, oblivious to the other conver-
sations.)

SYLVIA (defensively). I can't take the system so
seriously. (Holds up papers.) Did you get
these absurdities--"Lateness due to Absence,"
"High under-achiever," "Polio consent slips"?

BEA. I can match yours any day. (Reading.)
"Please disregard the following."

(SADIE FINCH has appeared on the platform.)

SADIE. All teachers. At the end of home room
period, send those students who have failed to
report for check out because they've left the
building to Mr. McHabe. (Going.)

SYLVIA (to BEA). How do we send students who've
left the building?

BEA (smiling as she goes). It'll be a challenge.

(CHARLOTTE WOLF has appeared on the platform.)

CHARLOTTE (to SYLVIA: severely). I'm forced to
cancel your library lessons on mythology. Your
students create havoc. They have no respect
for the printed page. Two of them took out
books indiscriminately.

SYLVIA. What better way to show respect than
by----

CHARLOTTE (interrupting; close to tears). Not
only that--they misplaced *The Golden Age of
Greece*, and they put Bullfinch on the Zoology
shelf!

(Sniffling, CHARLOTTE goes, while MR. BESTER
appears at another place on the platform.)

MR. BESTER. Miss Barrett--I plan to observe
your class soon.

SYLVIA (nervously). I see. Oh, Mr. Bester. The
bookroom has only eleven copies of *Romeo and
Juliet*.

MR. BESTER (going). Use *Ivanhoe*. They have a
hundred and sixty *Ivanhoes*.

(ELLA FRIEDENBERG has appeared.)

ELLA. I have some useful material for you, Miss
Barrett--a few more Personality Profiles. Lou
Martin exhibits inverted hostility in manic behavior patterns. Eddie Williams must curb
paranoia due to socio-economic environmental
factors.

SYLVIA. What am I to do with that information?

ELLA (going right on). My biggest concern is Joe
Ferone. A dangerous situation. Explosive.
It's imperative to channel his libidino-aggres-
sive impulses into socially acceptable attitudes.

SYLVIA. How? What do you suggest?

(FRANCES EGAN has put her head in.)

FRANCES. Diet. Nutrition. Make sure he has a
hot breakfast.

SYLVIA. I'm not his mother.

ELLA (to FRANCES, who goes). Stay out of this.
(Back to SYLVIA.) He cuts classes. Disrupts
others. Every stairway is clearly marked--an
up stairway, or a down stairway. He always
goes opposite. (Going.) You'll have to do
something!

(MC HABE, holding JOE FERONE firmly by the
    arm, has come in L, and stands just inside
    door.)

MC HABE (straining to keep his anger in control).
    Miss Barrett--will you come here, please?
SYLVIA (recognizing trouble; rising). Oh, dear----
    (Speaking to class as she crosses.) Concentrate
    on your papers. (As she approaches MC HABE;
    keeping her voice low.) What is it? (MC HABE
    is utterly outraged, but because of the covertly
    watching students, both he and SYLVIA speak in
    hushed voices.)
MC HABE. How dare you?
SYLVIA. How dare I what?
MC HABE. Let him out of the room unescorted?
SYLVIA. He had to go.
MC HABE. Unescorted?
SYLVIA. There was no hall proctor.
MC HABE. You should have waited.
SYLVIA. The situation did not warrant waiting.
MC HABE. His exam paper may be invalidated.
SYLVIA (uncowed). Why?
MC HABE (it's harder to control his anger). He may
    have been looking up answers.
SYLVIA. He told me he wouldn't.
MC HABE. He told you?
SYLVIA. Yes.
MC HABE (incredulous). And you believed him?
SYLVIA (strong). I believed him. (MC HABE has to
    catch his breath before he can go on.)
MC HABE (to JOE). Go back to your seat, young
    man.
SYLVIA (as JOE goes back to his seat; repeating). I
    believe him.
MC HABE (gestures). Girl in fourth seat--eyes on
    your paper! (To SYLVIA.) Will you come here,

please. (He has stepped out of classroom into
area at L. SYLVIA is following him to just outside her classroom door.)

SYLVIA. Yes, Mr. McHabe.

MC HABE (goaded but still hushed). This isn't the
time or the place to explain to you the gravity
of your position. You had explicit instructions.
You disobeyed them. When Ferone finishes,
put his paper aside.

SYLVIA. He did not cheat.

MC HABE (a hushed explosion). They don't need
your coddling; they need discipline. We have
to punish them--punish them for every infrac-
tion--because if we don't, they'll get it later
from a cop or a judge. Ever been in a juvenile
court? Sure, we've got to win their respect,
but there's just one way--strict enforcement!
(Takes breath.) There's a strong possibility
your end term rating will be an unsatisfactory!
(Turns. Points.) See what they're doing. Keep
track of them. (He goes out L. SYLVIA turns,
shattered, trying to collect herself, and crosses back to her desk. She glances at the students.
None of them smile, or try to be funny. Almost
deliberately they turn back to their papers.
SYLVIA takes a deep breath, walks back to her
desk and sits. The students are busy, im-
passive.)

SYLVIA (quietly). When the bell sounds, please
bring your examination papers to my desk.

CHARLES (rising; with a tone of respect). I finished early, Miss Barrett. (She nods and he
brings his paper to her.) Actually I do write
left-handed sometimes.

SYLVIA. Thank you, Charles. (LOU is also coming forward with his paper.)

LOU (his best manners). Hope I did okay, Miss

Barrett.

SYLVIA. I'm sure you did, Lou. (ALICE has come forward with her paper.)

ALICE. I mixed up my homework papers. (Hushed.) Thank you for sticking up for me--for us. (The bell rings. The others, except JOE who continues to write quickly, get up and start forward with their papers. As the surprised SYLVIA is beginning to realize, there's a change in their manner.)

LINDA (respectfully). It was a hard test, Miss Barrett, but that's not your fault. (After turning in papers, they exit L.)

CARRIE. Here's mine, Miss Barrett.

RACHEL. Now you have to mark them. Such a long day for you, teach.

CAROLE (digging her in ribs). Talk nice.

RACHEL (quickly correcting). Miss Barrett.

JILL. Everything's gonna be fine.

HARRY. If it was up to me, I'd say you're very satisfactory.

VIVIAN. Don't mind him, Miss Barrett.

RUSTY (to HARRY, as they go). Big mouth.

ELIZABETH (going). You had us very well prepared, thank you.

LENNIE (wanting to please her). Maybe Homer isn't really such a lousy writer. If you say so, I'll give him another try.

SYLVIA (smiling). It's optional, Lennie.

LENNIE (considering). In that case--I'll--I'll see. (SYLVIA smiles after the departing LENNIE. As he goes, she's left alone with JOE, who still sits at his desk and is now staring at her. The smile fades. JOE gets up, brings his paper to her desk and tosses it down.)

JOE (bitterly). You may fool them, but you don't fool me. You're even phonier than the others

because you put on this act--being a dame you
know how--pretending you give a damn! (His
voice rising.) Just who do you think you're
kidding? (He glares at her, then turns abruptly
and starts back L. As he approaches the door,
he slows down and then stops just inside the
door, his back to SYLVIA.)

SYLVIA (quietly). Anything else, Joe?

JOE (without turning; angry and unhappy). Nothing
else. Nothing. Too bad I can't believe you,
that's all.

(As JOE goes out L, ELLEN comes on the platform,
holding a letter.)

ELLEN (calling back as she comes). It's from Sylvia.
She says she's beginning to think she isn't com-
municating with anyone. (Speaking directly to
SYLVIA.) You better communicate with Mattie.
How are you going to answer her letter about
the February vacancy at Willowdale? (SYLVIA
shrugs.) Tell me about Willowdale.

SYLVIA. It's a small suburban college. (Wistful.)
Pleasant, cozy. Mattie writes they have trees
in the windows. (Chuckles.) And sit in leather
chairs and sip coffee.

(DR. MAXWELL CLARKE has appeared at the other
side of the platform.)

DR. CLARKE. Miss Barrett.

SYLVIA (rising). Yes, Dr.Clarke?

DR. CLARKE. It has come to my attention that due
to laxness on your part, one of our students is
under suspicion of cheating. This can have a
demoralizing and corrupting effect, and I find
your actions upsetting and disturbing.

SYLVIA (subdued). Yes, Dr. Clarke.

DR. CLARKE. Incidentally, in looking over your
    record, I see a note from the payroll depart-
    ment about a salary overpayment of two dol-
    lars and seventy-five cents for last June.
    (Sternly.) That overpayment should have been
    taken care of long ago.

SYLVIA (as she realizes; after him). But I wasn't
    even here in June. I didn't start till----(But
    he is gone.)

ELLEN (it's time for SYLVIA to get sensible).
    Sylvia--is there any reason for not applying to
    Willowdale?

SYLVIA. No reason, except----

ELLEN. Except what?

(ALICE is coming on L, nervous, looking back over
    her shoulder.)

SYLVIA. Except I like high school kids. I chose to
    teach here. No one forced me--it was my
    choice. And in spite of everything, I've got to
    keep trying.

ELLEN (half teasing). You feel your reach should
    exceed your grasp?

ALICE (calling from classroom doorway). Miss
    Barrett.

SYLVIA (sees ALICE; back to ELLEN as though
    finishing a letter). Have to close. I'll phone
    tomorrow night--after eight.

ELLEN (reading letter). "Love, Sylvia." (Realiz-
    ing.) That phone call should have come tonight.
    (Going. Concerned.) I wonder what happened.

ALICE. Miss Barrett--I need help.

SYLVIA. What's the matter?

ALICE. I did something so stupid! I could die!

SYLVIA. What is it?

ALICE. The letter.
SYLVIA. What letter?
ALICE (in pain). To Mr. Barringer.
SYLVIA (pushing her into a chair). Alice--sit down.
    (Trying to sort this out.) You sent a letter to
    Mr. Barringer?
ALICE. You have to get it back. I mean, any mi-
    nute he might----
SYLVIA. I can't do that.
ALICE (too upset to listen). It's in room 309. On
    his desk. There was no one around and I left it
    on his desk.
SYLVIA. Well, go over to 309 and----
ALICE. I'm afraid. (Hushed.) Suppose he's there?
    Suppose he's read it? How could I face him?
SYLVIA (puzzled by the extent of her upset). What's
    in the letter?
ALICE. It was a terrible mistake.
SYLVIA (softly). Then get it back. Just go.
ALICE.   I can't!

(At this same moment, PAUL is coming on L, carry-
    ing a letter.)

PAUL (seeing ALICE). There you are. (Clears
    throat.) I received your letter----
ALICE (swallowing). Yes?
PAUL. I want to talk to you about this letter.
ALICE (with a stir of hope; perhaps she's reached
    him). You do?
PAUL (gesturing for her to come). I'd like to see
    you privately.
ALICE (the stir of hope a little stronger; starting L;
    hushed). See me? Privately?
PAUL (to SYLVIA). Excuse us, please. (SYLVIA
    nods, crossing back to her desk, where she
    sits.)

ALICE (as she precedes PAUL out the classroom
    door into the area to L). Yes, Mr.----(Stops
    herself, and starts to say "Paul," but she
    doesn't quite dare. Her hope is growing.)
    You want to talk about my letter?
PAUL (nodding). And make a few corrections.
ALICE (bewildered). Corrections?
PAUL (nodding again; professionally). You use a
    series of dots instead of punctuation. Let's see,
    now. (Reads quickly and without expression.)
    Dear Mr. Barringer. Last Sunday I took the
    subway to your stop--insert comma--having
    looked it up on your time card dot dot dot. I
    hope you don't mind the presumption. (Looks
    up.) That's misspelled. (ALICE swallows with
    difficulty. This isn't what she expected. He
    continues rapidly and without expression.) I
    walked back and forth across the street from
    your house--insert comma--back and forth--
    insert comma--and my heart was throbbing with
    this love I bear for you dot dot dot. (Looks up
    again.) "Throbbing" is a cliché. (ALICE is too
    disturbed to speak. He continues, as before.)
    I think of you all the time dot dot dot. I pray to
    be worthy of you. (ALICE is stunned and mute.)
    And if ever you need me to die for you, I will
    gladly do so dot dot dot. (ALICE starts slowly
    L. Unconscious of this, he continues.) I feel so
    deeply the truth and beauty--clichés, no need to
    capitalize. But I have to speak out this love I
    feel dot dot dot dot dot----(He looks up to see her
    going. Speaking after her.) There are some
    repetitions here and a change of tense, along
    with----(But she's gone. He looks after her
    with a moment of concern, then shrugs and goes
    back into Sylvia's classroom.)
SYLVIA (as he comes in, she stands; deeply

concerned; in a low voice). What did you do?

PAUL (defensively). I handled her letter the only possible way.

SYLVIA. How?

PAUL. As a composition.

SYLVIA. Oh, no.

PAUL. Yes. (More defensive. Shrugs, anxious to pass it off.) What does a neurotic adolescent know about love?

SYLVIA (with quiet anger). Probably much more than you know about a nuclear physicist marooned on Kamchatka. (PAUL starts to reply, but he can't. He turns abruptly and walks out L. The anger goes out of SYLVIA. She suddenly feels defeated. She sits at her desk again, picks up her pen, and puts a piece of paper in position to write. She considers the paper a moment, and then starts writing, saying the words as she writes them.) I understand there may be a vacancy at Willowdale Academy in February, and it is in this connection that I'm writing to you. (A bell starts ringing in short bursts. SYLVIA looks up at this and then goes back to her letter as the bell stops. Repeating.) That I'm writing to you. I hold a license in English in the New York City----

(BEA has appeared on the platform.)

BEA (concerned). Sylvia--do you know what the commotion is about outside?

SYLVIA. What commotion?

BEA (as she goes). Something's going on.

(KATHERINE hurries in L.)

KATHERINE (demanding). Miss Barrett--have you
  seen Mr. Barringer? He's wanted right away.
SYLVIA. He left just a moment ago.
KATHERINE. Where to?
SYLVIA. No idea.
KATHERINE (hurrying off L). If he comes back,
  tell him call the office. Immediately!
SYLVIA (after her). I don't expect to----
  (KATHERINE is gone. SYLVIA turns back to
  her letter, determined to finish.) A license
  in English in the New York City Secondary
  Schools and am at present teaching at Calvin----

  (FRANCES EGAN appears on the platform.)

FRANCES (to SYLVIA; crisis). Please send down
  the Health card for Alice Blake--urgent. Do
  you have any blank accident reports? I'm all
  out--urgent!
SYLVIA. No, I don't. Has there been an accident?
  What's----

(But FRANCES is gone. MC HABE has appeared
  on the platform.)

MC HABE. All teachers and students will remain
  in their rooms disregarding the bells until
  further notice. Lessons are to proceed as
  usual with no reference to the incident.
  Teachers are to discourage morbid curiosity.
SYLVIA. Mr. McHabe? What incident? What
  happened?

(MC HABE is gone. A siren begins faintly in the
  distance. FRAN hurries on L. ELLA appears
  on platform.)

ELLA (deeply upset). Such behavior is completely
      atypical for a girl with such a stable Person-
      ality Profile. (Going.) But there are factors
      beyond our control.
FRAN (to SYLVIA). The office wants you to fill out
      this Emergency Form.
SYLVIA (sharply). I don't know anything about an
      emergency.
FRAN (putting form in front of her; helpfully). All
      you do--check one. Parent or Guardian.
      Reached. Not reached. By telephone. By
      telegram. Opposite parent or guardian of--
      fill in Alice Blake. Then after we regret to
      inform you, fill in----
SYLVIA. Fill in what? Tell me!
FRAN (surprised). Don't you know? (The siren is
      getting louder.)
SYLVIA. Is that the police or is it----
FRAN. Probably the ambulance. To take Alice
      Blake to the hospital. She fell out of a window.
      (SYLVIA gasps. The light begins to dim.
      FRAN, back to business:) Okay. Now. The
      office wants you to fill out this form. (As the
      light is dimming off, FRAN demands SYLVIA's
      attention to the business at hand. She continues
      patiently.) Please check one. Parent or
      Guardian. Reached. Not reached. By tele-
      phone. By telegram. To parent or guardian--
      please fill in----

(The light has dimmed to black. The sound of the
      siren climaxes and stops. In the darkness,
      the curtain falls.)

ACT TWO

SCENE: A bell rings and the curtain rises revealing the set as before except for one change. The cut-outs on the platform at L and R now have the words "Suggestion Box" printed on them.

The blackboard in Miss Barrett's classroom has a recent lesson on it including a diagramed sentence, a note encouraging students to pick up a supplementary reading list from Miss Barrett's desk, and a message that reads: "Miss B. I'm here so don't count me absent. The reason I'm not here is because I'm in the office. Carole. "

A spot of light illuminates each of the two "Suggestion Box" areas, with a minimum of light presently on the rest of the stage.

AT RISE OF CURTAIN: DR. CLARKE is discovered in the center of the platform. On the lower level, at DRC, SADIE FINCH and ELLA FRIEDENBERG are discovered looking up respectfully to DR. CLARKE.

DR. CLARKE (clears throat). All teachers. I have noted and observed in assembly that a number of our students seem uncertain of the words of our alma mater song, "The Purple

and Gold. " Teachers are advised to go over
the wording with their students. Singing our
alma mater with the right and proper feeling
should foster and encourage a more appropri-
ate school spirit and public image. The words
of the first stanza are as follows:

> Ye loyal sons and daughters
> Whose hearts will ne'er grow old
> As long as ye are true to
> The purple and gold.

(Going.) Thank you.

(As he concludes, SADIE and ELLA start L.)

ELLA (smiling). Maybe that will solve everything.
SADIE. If they're going to sing the alma mater,
     sing it correctly. (Noticing, catching ELLA's
     arm.) Look at that.
ELLA. At what?
SADIE. Suggestion Box! Miss Barrett's installed
     suggestion boxes!
ELLA (surprised). She's asking for it.
SADIE. It's almost the end of the term. Why start
     innovations now?
ELLA. Because she can't wait. She's a masochist.
     (Shaking head as they go off L.)   That's a high
     school teacher who sets up a suggestion box.

(As they complete exit L, CHARLES stands up at the
     right side of the platform as though coming out
     of that "Suggestion Box. ")

NOTE: *After he speaks, he steps down quickly and
     then another student apparently comes out of the
     other suggestion box, and so forth. They appear
     one after the other without delay, but not so rap-
     idly as to cut off audience reaction to the previous*

line.

CHARLES. Teachers are always telling what's
     wrong with us, what about the other way around?
     I wish they all had suggestion boxes. Boy,
     would I like to tell them off! But you're okay,
     Miss Barrett . . . for a teacher. You said we
     gotta have the courage of our convictions and
     sign our name, but we don't have to--so I'm not.

(As he goes, LINDA stands up at left suggestion box.)

LINDA. Not enough boys and too many girls. But
     that's not your fault. Also some schools they
     have dancing in the cafeteria and they put on
     different things, why not. You only live once.
     Linda Rosen.
EDWARD. Abolish prejudice! Abolish Miss Fried-
     enberg's interviews! They make me sick, like
     when she asked am I ashamed where I live.
     Edward Williams, Esquire.
CARRIE. I don't like the way you dress. Too loud
     for a teacher. You should tone it down. And
     you're a low marker. Signed: Your Enemy.
LENNIE (NOTE: He says "writting"). Teachers
     are ruining America! This is the last time
     I'm writting. Signed: The Hawk.
VIVIAN. You seem to be a very understandable
     person. By that I mean you understand us not
     being so old yourself. Too bad you're a teach-
     er and pretty like my sister. I wish you were
     a plain person. Then we could be close. Vivian
     Paine.
RUSTY. The way you read is too emoting, and you
     have pets--like Joe Ferone. He must be your
     pet because he gives you so much trouble.
     Signed: Neglected.

JILL. You're a good teacher except for the rotten
    books you have to teach like the *Odyssey*. I
    wouldn't give it to a dog to read. Signed:
    Disgusted.
CAROLE. Is it okay if I start collecting money from
    the home room kids to send flowers to Alice
    Blake in the hospital? The thing is we always
    used to sit in front of each other. Carole Blanca.
LOU. On Mondays what do you think we are, orators?
    Signed: Mark Anthony.
HARRY (standing beside LOU). It is my considered
    opinion that you are very well qualified. No
    matter how boring the lesson, you always make
    it interesting. I suggest you continue the good
    work. Harry A. Kagan.
LOU (as HARRY is giving name, LOU pushes him
    aside). Clean up the slums--before you go to
    Mars! And stop the bomb--before it's too late!
    As far as school, without us there could be no
    school, ha ha. And no futures! Lou Martin.
RACHEL. Please tell Lou Martin to quit showing
    off. He thinks he's so comic. Well, I don't.
    Signed: Serious Student.
LOU (poking his head in again). Have no fear, Miss
    Barrett. We're behind you sixty-five per cent.
ELIZABETH. Thank you for showing me that there
    is nothing more important than communication,
    but with so many other students, I feel we are
    both wasted. Elizabeth Ellis.
JOSE. I'm not a good penman, but I must tell some-
    one--I mean, I'd like someone to know. I'm
    putting this in the Suggestion Box for the record.
    (Takes a breath.) Today is my birthday. Happy
    Birthday. Signed: Me.

(As JOSE is going, PAUL BARRINGER is coming on
    DR at the lower level and well downstage. He is

going over something he's written--counting the
meter. BEA comes in DL, and is crossing toward him.)

BEA. You've written something brilliant again?
PAUL. A parody of Ezra Pound in many cantos--
which I plan to lay at the feet of our dedicated
colleague. (Concerned.) Is Sylvia back in
school today?
BEA. Yes.
PAUL. Where'd she go yesterday?
BEA. I haven't spoken to her.
PAUL. I'm the villain. (Bothered.) How would
you handle a love letter from a student?
BEA. I've no idea.

(CHARLOTTE is coming on DR.)

CHARLOTTE. Is Sylvia back? (As they meet; a bit
uncomfortable.) I have a problem about Alice
Blake. She's still listed in Sylvia's official
class, and----
PAUL (on edge). What's the problem?
CHARLOTTE. An overdue book. She owes the
library forty-nine cents.
PAUL. What book?
CHARLOTTE (looking at slip of paper). *The Idylls
of the King.* Alfred Lord Tennyson.
BEA (pleasantly). You could always send a posse to
the hospital.
CHARLOTTE. I feel like a ghoul. But this is a
matter of record. And not the first time. I had
to warn her constantly about overdue books.
PAUL. Doesn't it get you a little excited that a
student really cares to read?
CHARLOTTE. You sound like Sylvia. (Strong.) I
used to get excited. But with no help, no books,
and constant demands, all I care about now is

for some shred of library to survive.

PAUL (reaching into his pocket). And right now you need forty-nine cents?

CHARLOTTE. Right now I'm caught with trying to maintain the rules I didn't make. But if paying the forty-nine cents would make you feel better----

PAUL (bitterly). I wish it were that easy.

CHARLOTTE. I remember your comments in the teachers' lounge. Getting involved does them no good. *Sauve qui peut.* Think only of yourself. Amused detachment, you said--that's the only way to remain intact.

PAUL. I'm not sure it's possible to teach and also remain intact.

CHARLOTTE (going L). Make up your mind.

PAUL (after her). As Ella Friedenberg would say-- I have a problem.

BEA (encouraging). But you're working on it.

(SYLVIA is entering DR.)

PAUL (putting himself down). All I really care about is maintaining my amused detachment.

BEA. Come off it, Paul.

PAUL (ingratiatingly to SYLVIA). I have another parody for you. Gray's "Elegy."
    The school bell tolls the knell of starting day.
    Ah, do not ask for whom it tolls! I see
    The students stairwards push their scream-
        ing way.
    I know, alas, it tolls for thee and me!

SYLVIA (quietly). That's very clever.

PAUL. I have some others here, also very clever. When I didn't see you yesterday, I was afraid you'd left us. (Embarrassed; going.) Glad you're back.

BEA. I think he's a lot more upset than he shows.
SYLVIA. Perhaps. (Concerned.) I couldn't even
    talk to Alice. She's not having visitors.
BEA. That's what I hear.

        (SADIE is appearing on the platform.)

SADIE (sharply). Miss Barrett. Why have you
    neglected to send in the attendance sheet for
    today?
SYLVIA. Because Linda Rosen wore a pink sweater
    and fuchsia stretch pants to school. She was
    seen by Mr. McHabe, who had her cool her
    heels in the office. She was also seen by the
    boys in my home room, who migrated en masse
    to her vicinity. I'll take attendance later--un-
    less they follow her like lemmings into the sea
    and are all drowned.
SADIE (going). I'll inform Mr. McHabe.
SYLVIA (to BEA). She had only one comment about
    Alice's accident----(Mimicking.) "Hand in be-
    fore three, locker number and book receipts for
    Blake, Alice." McHabc tells us to keep our
    public image intact and our students in their
    seats. Dr. Clarke urges us to be aware of our
    responsibility in a democracy.
BEA. What else can they say?
SYLVIA. I don't know. Some indication they care
    about the girl. Are we supposed to be uninvolved?

        (FRANCES appears on the platform.)

FRANCES. There was nothing any of us could have
    done for Alice. She was having a very rough
    time outside.
SYLVIA. How do you know?
FRANCES. Once she came to me beaten black and

blue.

SYLVIA. Beaten! What did you do?

FRANCES. Gave her a cup of tea.

SYLVIA. Tea? Why tea?

FRANCES. What else could I do? (Angry.) I know more than anyone here about what goes on outside--poverty, disease, malnutrition. Yet I'm not supposed to give them even a band-aid.

SYLVIA (indignant). But that's----

FRANCES (cutting in). Isn't it? I used to plead, bang on my desk, talk myself hoarse arguing with kids, parents, welfare administration, social agencies. Nobody even heard me! So I give them a cup of tea.

SYLVIA. But you're a nurse.

FRANCES (bitterly). Have you read the directive posted on my wall? (Quoting; emphatically.) "The school nurse may not touch wounds, give medication, remove foreign particles from the eye." And so on! And so on!

SYLVIA. I didn't realize----

FRANCES. So I hand out cups of tea and send around notes--poor nutrition is frequently the cause of poor marks. I don't know if anyone pays the slightest attention, but that's it for me--that's what I can do. (FRANCES would like to say more, but she can't. She goes. SYLVIA, somewhat shaken, looks after her.)

BEA (gently). None of us is God. Nothing is our fault--except, perhaps, poor teaching.

SYLVIA. Are we teaching? Is anything getting through? Or are we just talking to ourselves?

BEA. You were missed yesterday. I had to go down and rescue your substitute. Your kids were turning her into a nervous wreck.

SYLVIA. Why would they do that?

BEA. Misguided loyalty.

SYLVIA (surprised). To me?

BEA. You wouldn't believe the lesson, anyway. She was having them turn great poems into newspaper headlines.

SYLVIA. Such as?

BEA. "Midnight Rider Warns of Foe." "Seaman Guilty of Shooting Bird."

SYLVIA (smiling). "Wife Tells All in Portuguese Love Letters"?

BEA. Not bad. "Man Reports Talking Raven."

SYLVIA. Maybe I should stay away.

BEA. Where were you?

SYLVIA (concerned). I have a feeling my end term rating is going to be a big fat "U."

(MC HABE is entering DL.)

BEA. No one is rated unsatisfactory unless certified looney.

MC HABE. That's not entirely true, Mrs. Schachter. (Turns.) Regarding your requisition, Miss Barrett. We are all out of erasers. All out of red pencils. Our order for window poles was sent to the Board last spring--we must be patient. There's been an epidemic of chalk stealing. Please keep chalk under lock except when in use. (Hopefully.) However, we have some left-over posters. Yellow on green "Truth is Beauty." Also black on white "Learning equals Earning."

SYLVIA. What I really need----

MC HABE. We have to be patient. One thing more-- a frivolous attitude and levity of tone toward attendance-taking are unsuitable to the high seriousness of our profession.

SYLVIA. I'll try to cut down on the levity, Mr.

McHabe. Have you had a chance yet to go over Joe Ferone's examination paper?

MC HABE. Of course. So did Mr. Bester.

SYLVIA. I've been waiting to hear. I daresay Joe Ferone has, too.

MC HABE. His mark was 86.

SYLVIA. Any evidence of cheating?

MC HABE. You'd have heard.

SYLVIA. No evidence of cheating?

MC HABE. That's right.

SYLVIA. Shouldn't something be said--if not to me, at least to Joe Ferone?

MC HABE. Why?

SYLVIA. I'm hoping he'll stay in school.

MC HABE. He should not have been let out unescorted. He knew it and you knew it. The fact that he didn't cheat----

SYLVIA (cutting in). Should be noted.

MC HABE. To what purpose?

SYLVIA. No one likes to feel unsatisfactory.

MC HABE. If you're concerned about getting a "U"----

SYLVIA. I'm concerned about so many things, Mr. McHabe.

MC HABE. And you think you can handle the Joe Ferones? You try running the school for one day--you'll have a riot in every room.

SYLVIA. All I'm asking--some strong things were said. Now we know he did well. And since it was entirely on his own----

MC HABE. This time.

SYLVIA. I'd like there to be a next time.

MC HABE (going L; impatient). We'll always have more than we can handle. We have to be realistic. (Pauses.) You weren't here yesterday.

SYLVIA. I spent the day at Willowdale Academy. Being interviewed for a possible February job.

MC HABE (subdued). I see.

SYLVIA. I was being realistic.

MC HABE (going). Yes. Yes, of course.

BEA (looking after him; surprised). You upset him.

SYLVIA. McHabe?

BEA (nodding). He's upset.

SYLVIA. Not McHabe. Never.

BEA. Sylvia, I don't find him inspirational, either, but remember--his pupil load is three thousand!

SYLVIA. It's such a different world at Willowdale.

BEA. You mean nobody shouts "Hi, teach"?

SYLVIA. I mean I'd only have three classes a day, three times a week--the other two days for conferences. I might even give a seminar on Chaucer.

BEA. If that's what you want----

SYLVIA (strong). I want to practice my profession, that's all. I want to be like Chaucer's *Clerke of Oxford*--"Gladly would he learn and gladly teach."

BEA. Why do you think your students picked on the substitute yesterday?

SYLVIA. Ask McHabe.

BEA. Ask yourself. I have to get back.

SYLVIA (after her). Anything else happening here while I was gone?

BEA (pauses at L). Life was happening here.

(BEA goes out L. SYLVIA looks after her, then crosses to the blackboard and starts erasing it. As she does, her STUDENTS begin re-appearing out the suggestion boxes, one after the other. As they continue, SYLVIA sits to work at her desk.)

LOU. Don't worry, Miss Barrett. We're behind you eighty-five per cent.

LINDA. My mother has been living with me for sixteen years, but she still insists on cross-examining. Please talk to her. Signed: Linda.

RUSTY. I know school is supposed to help me with life, but so far it didn't. Rusty.

VIVIAN. Tell us more about your own life. It makes you feel very human. I'm only miserable at home and never in English. That's why I have this ambition to be an English teacher. Your friend. Vivian.

RACHEL. Teachers give tests for spite and to get even. You said we should sign our name. Signed: Anonymous.

EDWARD. When you call on me to answer, don't call on me when I don't know the answer. It makes me look dumb. You always call the others when they know the answer. Signed: Edward Williams, Esquire.

CAROLE. You have one of the best sense of humors I ever met. You make the lessons laughable. Carole.

ELIZABETH. Thank you for showing me that writing clearly means thinking clearly. Elizabeth.

LENNIE. Will you marry me? This is positively the last time I'm writting to you. Signed: The Hawk.

CHARLES. I enjoy the way your tone of voice makes poetry sound in changing it to sadness or happiness, depending on the poem. I went to the school library to look for more Robert Frost but it was closed. Charles. Sherry

JILL. You never call on me and if you do it's very seldom. Jill.

HARRY. I wish to commend you for taking an interest in mine and the class as a whole's grammar. Harry A. Kagan.

CARRIE. Cafeteria lunches are lousy. Your enemy.

JOSE. I'm nobody especial, so nobody knows me. But maybe if I drop out and get a job, I'll be somebody with a job. Signed: Me.

JOE (at left suggestion box; aggressive). Give me
one good reason why I should stay in school.
Signed: Joe Ferone. (SYLVIA has looked up
at this.)

SYLVIA. I can give you many good reasons.

JOE. To take what McHabe dishes out?

SYLVIA. It's time we talk this out. Stay after
school and----

JOE. What's in it for you?

SYLVIA (frankly). I'm beginning to wonder. For
the time being, let's just say it's my job.

JOE (half angry; going). If I didn't know better,
you'd even convince me. Save it for the sheep.

SYLVIA (after him). Joe, about our talk----(He's
gone.)

(PAUL BARRINGER appears at the other suggestion
box.)

PAUL (meekly). Miss Barrett.

SYLVIA (surprised; getting up and turning toward
him). Paul.

PAUL. I'm slipping this into your suggestion box as
the most likely place to catch your attention.

SYLVIA. You've got it.

PAUL. There's a rumor you're leaving the end of
the term. (Bothered.) Why on earth----

SYLVIA. Let's just say I couldn't find the proper
response to "Hi, teach."

PAUL. I wish you'd reconsider.

SYLVIA (curious). Why?

PAUL (half joking). Because if you leave, where
else would I get such ghastly honest literary
criticism?

SYLVIA (smiling). Are you sure you want criticism?

PAUL. No, but just the same--you're needed here.

You're our catalyst, spokesman, in-fighter.
Besides, you laugh good, like an English
teacher should. (Clears throat.) I'm not saying this to get a higher mark. Signed: Paul.

(As PAUL goes off R, ELLEN is coming in L on the
platform, reading out loud from a letter as she
comes.)

ELLEN (reading). "Paul invited me to an end-of-
the-term party but I just couldn't go. I mean,
how could I celebrate with a man who corrects
a love letter?" (To SYLVIA; directly.) You're
leaving for Willowdale anyway, so what's the
difference?

SYLVIA. The term ends this week. (Bothered.)
There was so much more I wanted to do.

ELLEN (humorously sarcastic). Such as have a
little talk with the Ferone boy and turn him into a model student?

SYLVIA. It's not a question of a model student. I
wouldn't want him to be that. I suppose Harry
Kagan's a model student--he's also a stuffed
shirt. There's so much more to Ferone, but
I can't seem to make any difference to him.
(Considering.) And that's why I want to teach;
that's probably the one and only compensation:
to make a permanent difference in the life of a
child.

ELLEN. In your first letter you quote a kid who
says she's better off out. As far as that school's
concerned, maybe you're better off out.

(MR. BESTER appears at another point on the platform.)

MR. BESTER. Miss Barrett, I'd like to speak to you.

SYLVIA (to ELLEN). Have to go. I'll write as soon
    as I can.
ELLEN (going). Don't forget.
SYLVIA (turning). Yes, Mr. Bester?

(As they talk, the STUDENTS come quietly into the
    classroom, take their seats, and apparently
    work on an assignment.)

MR. BESTER. I have some unofficial comments on
    your teaching--not those that will appear on my
    formal Observation Report.
SYLVIA (nervous). I see.
MR. BESTER. The lesson I observed was an inter-
    esting one. Was there a particular reason for
    choosing Robert Frost's "The Road Not Taken"?
SYLVIA. I wanted to lead them into a discussion of
    blazing a trail versus conformity, and to the
    regret inherent in any decision.
MR. BESTER. Certainly apropos.
SYLVIA (uncertain as to his meaning). Mr. Bester?
MR. BESTER. My comments follow. Ask your
    question first, then call the student by name--
    thus you engage the whole class in thinking.
    Avoid vague or loaded questions--"How do you
    feel about this poem?" Vague. "Do we regret
    what we haven't done?" The teacher obviously
    expects "yes."
SYLVIA. I see.
MR. BESTER. The boy next to me was doing his
    math. A teacher should move about the room.
    Immediate correction of English was effected,
    but you missed--"He should of took the road."
    "On this here road." And "he coon't make up
    his mind."
SYLVIA (smiling). Couldn't.
MR. BESTER. I like the way you handled the hostile

boy who came late, the one with the toothpick in his mouth. You made him feel the class had missed his contribution. But you should have made him remove the toothpick.

SYLVIA (with uneasy smile). I've been fighting a losing battle with that toothpick.

MR. BESTER. Well, win it. And don't let a few students monopolize the discussion. Call on the non-volunteers. I'm not sure you're putting your energy where it's most needed.

SYLVIA (unclear). Sir?

enter — MR. BESTER. The cream will probably rise to the top anyway. Where our help is most needed, Miss Barrett, is with the skim milk.

SYLVIA. I appreciate your criticism, Mr. Bester.

MR. BESTER (concerned). The lesson I observed was a fruitful discussion of choices. What really concerns me is your choice. But I see you have a class. (Going.) My formal report will follow.

(ELIZABETH has risen, holding a paper.)

ELIZABETH. Before we get to *Macbeth*, I have a piece of creative writing. (Reading; dramatically.) "I saw him scuttling like a crook, mak ing his fearful way, stealthy, among the dirty dishes crusted with grease, bearing food to his secret sons behind the drainboard. How fearful were his eyes. Shall I kill him?" (Matter-of-fact tone.) Miss Barrett, is it clear I'm writing about a cockroach?

SYLVIA. Crystal. But the subject is *Macbeth*.

ELIZABETH (as she sits; darkly). If you start to stifle me, too!

SYLVIA. I want to hear from some others. Do you have your homework on *Macbeth*? (CARRIE

is waving her hand. SYLVIA is delighted.)
Carrie! Good! I've been waiting all term for
you to raise your hand. What's your question?

CARRIE. Do you wear contact lenses?

SYLVIA (reproachfully). Only when I read *Macbeth*.
Have you read the scene for today?

CARRIE. Not all the way. I mean, you already know
who did it.

SYLVIA. Let's start at the beginning.

HARRY. Right. The way I see it----

SYLVIA. Charles.

CHARLES. The title is called *Macbeth*.

SYLVIA. The title is.

CHARLES. *Macbeth*.

SYLVIA. Didn't you read it last term in English?

CHARLES. I ain't never read it before.

SYLVIA. I've never read it.

CHARLES. Me neither. In this book the author
depicks.

SYLVIA. Depicts.

CHARLES. This murder.

SYLVIA. We were discussing the theme, not the
plot. What's the difference--Linda?

LINDA. The plot is what they do. The theme is how.

SYLVIA. Not exactly. Vivian?

VIVIAN. The theme is what's behind it.

SYLVIA. Behind what?

VIVIAN. The plot.

RUSTY. Mrs. Macbeth noodges him.

SYLVIA. You mean nudges?

RUSTY. Noodges. Being a female she spurns him
on.

SYLVIA. Edward?

EDWARD. Edward Williams, Esquire.

SYLVIA. Esquire.

EDWARD. The theme is he kills him for his own
good.

SYLVIA (shakes head). Jose.

JOSE. Me?

SYLVIA. Yes. You. Well, Jose?

JOSE (embarrassed). I didn't have my hand up.

SYLVIA. But I'm calling on you.

JOSE (his nervousness growing). Why me, Miss
    Barrett?

SYLVIA (gently). Did you read it, Jose?

JOSE. Yes, but----

SYLVIA. What would you say is the theme?

JOSE. I didn't volunteer. My hand wasn't raised.

SYLVIA. We'd like your opinion.

HARRY. If you ask me----

SYLVIA. Not this time, Harry.

JILL. If you want the theme. Well, in my opinion,
    I think----

SYLVIA. I've asked Jose. (Turns back to him;
    smiling; encouraging.) Jose?

JOSE (takes a breath; with an effort). The author
    tries to say----

SYLVIA. Tries? Doesn't he succeed?

JOSE. He tries to show----

SYLVIA. He shows.

JOSE. He shows you mustn't be--be ambitious.

SYLVIA. Does he say ambition is bad?

CAROLE. Yes. Very bad.

SYLVIA. Jose. Isn't it good to be ambitious?

JOSE. Yes----(Struggling.) But not too.

SYLVIA. Not too what?

JOSE. Too ambitious is not so good.

SYLVIA. You mean, excessive ambition----

JOSE (with sudden decision). Can lead to big trouble.
    That's the theme.

SYLVIA (with a glow of pleasure). That's right.
    You're right, Jose.

JOSE (still uncertain). I was right?

SYLVIA (delighted). Yes.

JOSE. I figured out the theme, right?

SYLVIA (nodding). I have to call on you more often.

JOSE. Why not? (Half bravado, half confidence.)
Why not? (There is then a burst of simultaneous voices from all over the classroom, hands
up at the same time, and everyone but JOE
talking.)

STUDENTS (together). Now my turn! Call on me!
Oh, please! My opinion about *Macbeth*----
What Shakespeare is portraying----My turn----
The main thing in *Macbeth*----Miss Barrett----
Excessive and ruthless ambition----My hand
was up first----Hey, Miss Barrett----Teach!
(In the midst of this, the bell rings.)

SYLVIA (smiling). Saved by the bell. (There's a
groan of frustration.) Out with you. (They're
going.)

RACHEL. Any time I have something to say, the
bell rings.

VIVIAN. Because it's a short class.

CAROLE. Jose, the brain.

JOSE. Don't knock it. (To CAROLE as they go.)
Any time you want to know about themes----

RUSTY (going). The real villain--Mrs. Macbeth.

LOU. I say he was led on by the witches. Right at
the top, they egg him on.

LENNIE (following them out). Bubble, Bubble--toil
and trouble .

EDWARD. What-a they know about toil and trouble?

RUSTY. Remember when she hollers "out, damn
spot"? If she'd kept her mouth shut----(As
they troop out L, SYLVIA becomes aware of
JOE FERONE, who is still sitting quietly in
his seat.)

SYLVIA. The bell, Joe. School's out.

JOE. I heard.

SYLVIA. Is there something?

JOE. You've kept asking me to stay for a talk.
    Okay--I've stayed. Here I am. How about
    that?
SYLVIA (realizing this is the showdown; rising;
    soberly). I see.
JOE (challenging). What do ya wanta say? Let's
    go. Let's have it.
SYLVIA. I've been going over your entire record,
    Joe. I'm struck by the discrepancy between
    your capacity and your achievement.
JOE. Would you mind putting that in----
SYLVIA (cutting in). English? How about "I don't
    understand them big words, teach?" And you
    could keep asking me to repeat. You could
    drop some books. You could rock on your
    heels. You could----
JOE (to stop her). Okay!
SYLVIA. This is important, Joe. To both of us.
JOE. My discrepancies?
SYLVIA. Your capacity.
JOE (demanding). What's it to you? Why should
    you care?
SYLVIA. I do.
JOE (considers; perhaps he can let himself believe).
    That's what you told me before----
SYLVIA (hope making her eager). Come back for
    next term. Don't drop out. Joe, listen----
JOE (meaningfully). Are you listening?
SYLVIA. I'm trying to.
JOE (he's heard talk; his manner is over-casual).
    You gonna be here?
SYLVIA. Joe----
JOE (as she hesitates). That's a straight question.
SYLVIA (unhappy). Then I have to say no.
JOE (tightly). No what?
SYLVIA. I won't be here.
JOE (impassively repeating). You won't be here. I

see. Well, thanks, anyway.

SYLVIA. That doesn't mean----

JOE (cutting in, bitter with disappointment; he's been had again). We've finished our talk, Miss Barrett. (Pauses at door L, all the bitterness of his life in this disappointment.) What makes you think you're so special? (He goes out L.)

(The crushed SYLVIA sinks back down into her chair. BEA appears on the platform above and notices her.)

BEA (puzzled by SYLVIA). Sylvia----(SYLVIA looks up at her but can't bring herself to say anything. BEA is suddenly serious.) Are you all right?

SYLVIA (still in shock). I remember the first time I was able to excite my students about an idea. A lesson on Browning's "A man's reach should exceed his grasp or what's a heaven for?" (Wryly.) It made me feel special.

BEA. Are you reaching for something?

SYLVIA. I'm falling flat on my face.

BEA. What's happened?

SYLVIA. How do you stand up?

BEA. You're serious?

SYLVIA. Yes.

BEA. Walk through the halls. Listen at the classroom doors. In one--a lesson on the nature of Greek tragedy. In another--a drill on "who" and "whom." In another--a hum of voices intoning French conjugations. In another--silence; a math quiz.

SYLVIA. Yes, but what about----

BEA. Whatever the waste, stupidity, ineptitude, whatever the problems and frustrations, something exciting is going on. In each of the classrooms, all at the same time, education is going on--young people exposed to education. That's how I manage to stand up.

SYLVIA. Bea--am I a dropout?

BEA (genuinely). Don't be silly. You do what you feel is best.

SYLVIA. For the first time I've been seeing myself through the eyes of others.

BEA. Whose eyes?

SYLVIA. For one, Joe Ferone.

BEA. Get past the words, Sylvia, get to what they're really saying. I have to go. Another salvage problem.

SYLVIA. Thanks. (The light is dimming.)

BEA (SYLVIA is staring front again; she calls softly). Get to what they're really saying.

(As BEA goes, LINDA appears at the other side.)

LINDA. I don't know if you've noticed, Miss Barrett, but I decided to dress more conservative. And since coming to you I only wear eyelashes on dates.

(As LINDA goes, LOU appears at another point on the platform.)

LOU. When I turn seventeen my father says why should he feed an extra mouth. Ha ha, that's me. What I'm saying, Miss Barrett, is I hope I can come back.

(CAROLE appears.)

CAROLE. You helped me by giving me a liking for school which I previously lacked. If Alice was back in front of me she would sign her name, too, so I'll sign for her. Carole and Alice.

(JOSE appears.)

JOSE. English would be better off with more teach-
    ers like you that take an interest instead of just
    teaching due to circumstances. I'll never for-
    get you as long as I live. You made me feel
    I'm real. I used to sign "Me." But not any
    more. Jose Rodriguez.

(JOE appears.)

JOE. Miss Barrett! (She looks up to him. Hard,
    as before.) What makes you think you're so
    special? (She doesn't reply. He goes on.) Are
    you listening? (But a larger emotion is taking
    hold of him.) What I said--what I'm saying--
    I'm saying you're so special! You're my teach-
    er. So teach me. Help me. Hey, teach--which
    way do I go? I'm tired of going up the down
    staircase!

(During this last speech, the light dims to black. In
    the darkness, a bell rings. Then a spot appears
    on the center of the platform with DR. CLARKE
    standing in it.)

DR. CLARKE. Attention, please. This is your
    principal, Dr. Maxwell Clarke, and I wish to
    take this opportunity on the first morning of the
    first day of the February term to extend a warm
    welcome to all faculty and staff, and with the
    sincere and earnest hope we can go forward and
    upward together.

(If possible, a spot of light comes on the blackboard

and someone stands and writes on it in a bold
hand: "MISS BARRETT." General light is
coming up on the classroom and STUDENTS
are pouring in, much as they did at the beginning of the first act.)

LENNIE. Hey, she's back! Hurray, we got Barrett!
EDWARD. The only thing good about this place.
JOSE. Couldn't do without us, hey?
SYLVIA. That's right. Please take your seats.
RACHEL. What's the date?
HARRY. February, moron. (Turns to SYLVIA.)
     Happy to recontinue, Miss Barrett.
JILL. I'm not late. The bell's early.
SYLVIA. You'll have to fill out the new attendance
     cards.
VIVIAN. Who's got a pen?
LINDA. I hope we get a lot of new kids this term.
LENNIE. There's not enough seats.

(SADIE has appeared on platform, followed by others.)

SADIE. Disregard previous notice about disregard-
     ing the bells, please.
CHARLOTTE. The school library is your library.
     (Clears throat.) No students allowed into
     library until further notice.
VIVIAN. Hey, the window's still broke!
SYLVIA. We have to be patient. Now, if you'll pass
     these cards.
ELIZABETH. I hope we have you for creative writ-
     ing this term.
FRANCES (on platform). All members of faculty
     are to emphasize the importance of nutrition.
ELLA (also on platform). Personality Profiles in
     depth, please!
CAROLE. I'm glad you're back. That's from the

heart, not the mouth.

SYLVIA. Thank you. Now please----

(FRAN is entering.)

FRAN. I have a message from Mr. McHabe.
    You're to read it right away.
SYLVIA. Not till I've taken attendance.
FRAN. McHabe says----
SYLVIA. Mr. McHabe.
FRAN. Right away.
SYLVIA (taking papers; with quiet authority). After
    attendance.

(A STUDENT rushes in.)

SYLVIA. Good morning, Rusty. Why are you late?
RUSTY. I'm not late. I had my English changed.
    I wanted you.
SYLVIA. I'm glad. Well, find a place.

(KATHERINE has come in.)

KATHERINE. Miss Barrett. Mr. McHabe says----
SYLVIA. I'm about to take attendance.
KATHERINE. He says it's important.
SYLVIA. Later, Katherine. Attention, class. If I
    mispronounce any of the new names, please
    correct me. (Consulting list.) Arbuzzi, Helen.
    (Remembering.) No, that's wrong. She dropped
    out the start of last term.
HELEN (from back of class). No, it's right. I got
    a job--after school. I decided to give it another
    try.

(MC HABE appears on platform.)

SYLVIA (to HELEN). Me, too. (Back to list.)

Next----

MC HABE (thundering). Miss Barrett!

SYLVIA (looking up). Sir?

MC HABE. All I wanted to ask--could you use some of these posters? Blue on white, "Knowledge is Power." Green on yellow, "Learning equals Earning."

SYLVIA (considers an instant, then decides). I'd love some posters, Mr. McHabe.

MC HABE (delighted). Ah. Very good. Please-- continue with your attendance.

SYLVIA. Axelrod, Leon.

JILL. Him? He's always absent!

RUSTY. You're lucky he's not here!

EDWARD. Will he give you trouble!

SYLVIA. Arrons, Charles.

(CHARLES is coming forward.)

CHARLES (putting slip on her desk). You have to sign my book clearance.

SYLVIA (signing automatically). But----

CHARLES (taking slip and going). Thank you.

SYLVIA (after him; concerned). Charles, wait----

CHARLES. I'm dropping out, Miss Barrett.

SYLVIA (deeply disappointed; looking down at her attendance book, repeating as she makes note). Arrons, Charles. Dropped out.

(JOE FERONE has entered as she is making note, and is crossing toward her desk. SYLVIA hasn't seen him yet.)

JOE (speaking with decision). Mark me present, Miss Barrett. (She looks up, and for an instant they stare at each other.)

SYLVIA (this means a great deal to her, but she keeps

her manner casual). Joe Ferone. Present.
JOE (with his old arrogance; tossing paper on her
    desk). Here's this.
SYLVIA. Here's what?
JOE (shrugs). A book report.
SYLVIA (deciding to play it the same way he is).
    Well, that's no way to hand it to me.
JOE (starting back to desk). My aim is bad.
SYLVIA (after him). We'll have to work on it.
JOE. On what?
SYLVIA (meaningfully). Your aim.

(LOU rushes in.)

LOU. I made it! I'm back! Lou Martin is behind
    you ninety-five per cent. (He sits and sighs
    with pleasure.) Hi, teach.
SYLVIA (smiles back at him). Hi, pupe! (The
    curtain is falling. SYLVIA starts to call names
    from her book, to which voices respond "Here.")
    Acevedo, Fiore? Amdur, Janet? Belgado,
    Ramos?

THE CURTAIN IS DOWN

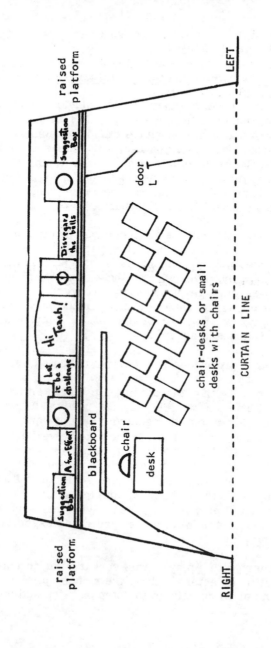

"Let it be a challenge!"

Production notes from the playwright.

The fictional high school of this play is an over-crowded understaffed New York City school with problems that are sometimes hilarious, sometimes heartbreaking. While many of the students who attend "Calvin Coolidge High" come from poor families, this is not a ghetto school. A lot of funny things happen here, but as one critic suggested, "It's the kind of 'funny' that hurts."

Underneath the comedy and humorous juxtapositions there's a real concern on the part of the faculty and students to teach and to be taught. Even so, it's much more interesting if these underlying good intentions emerge as the play progresses rather than be anticipated in the characterizations. Accordingly, we urge that each role be played with commitment and as written.

The stage directions are clearly indicated in the script, and they are easy to follow. It is important in doing this that the actor keep the intention in view. Examples: Ellen may be reading a letter, go from this into a dialogue with Sylvia, and then back to the letter. Joe Ferone may be verbalizing a "suggestion" and then go into a conversation. Mr. McHabe may go from a general announcement into an exchange with a teacher, and so forth. This shifting is clear in the play, and the actor or actress should play it as written. With this sort of free-flow, we achieve a fast-paced and especially exciting play.

Obviously with a play of this sort it's particularly helpful if the actors pick up their cues quickly -- though not so quickly as to "step on" the audience reaction to a previous line. One or two alert stage managers backstage could be quite helpful toward achieving a smooth and on-cue "traffic flow."

There is only one set in this play, but it makes an important contribution to the pace and humor of the show. It is diagramed on page 146 and described at the beginning of the play.   While the classroom portion of the set is straightforward, the producing group is invited to use their imagination in arranging and decorating the raised platform behind the classroom. The decorations, slogans, and various ways of presenting the actors on the platform are entirely optional except that access must be easy to avoid delays.

Now the play is in your hands.   Have a wonderful time with it.

NOTES ON CHARACTERS
AND COSTUMES

FACULTY

SYLVIA BARRETT: (Played by Sandy Dennis in the motion picture.) She is a very attractive and sensitive young teacher who is teaching her first class. She cares deeply about her profession, but she also has a wonderful sense of the absurd which is one way she hangs on to her sanity. She has a resilient enthusiasm, a genuine concern for her students, and ultimately great strength. Her clothes should be more "adult" than those worn by her students, especially since she is such a young teacher. While not expensive they should be quite good-looking.

PAUL BARRINGER: He is a very handsome English teacher and accordingly much admired, especially by his girl students. In a sense his refuge is in being an unpublished writer, apparently poised to flee the school the moment his writing is published. His fear of involvement makes him appear insensitive. He emphasizes his role of "author" by wearing worn tweed jackets.

BEATRICE SCHACHTER: She's a little older than Sylvia but much more experienced. In spite of having "been through the mill, " she retains a great zest both for teaching and for life. She is a natural "befriender" and she can't resist helping Sylvia in every way she can. She retains a humorous perspective and in the final scene with Sylvia, she makes one of the key speeches in the play. Her clothes are attractive, but a little older than Sylvia's.

J. J. MC HABE: "Administrative Assistant" is his title, but he's the disciplinary force that holds the school together. His manner is strong, sometimes angry, and at times he seems a would-be dictator. That would be an unfair judgment, however. Keeping this large school orderly is his job and he goes about it with blazing determination. Still, he is a complex person; for example, if his only concern was order, why does he keep urging teachers to use his supply of educational posters? The actor playing this role is urged to play it without compromise, and to allow the added dimensions of the character to emerge as they will in these unexpected ways. Mr. McHabe doesn't care about his clothes, usually wearing an unpressed business suit.

SADIE FINCH: She is the Chief Clerk and in a sense a feminine version of J.J. McHabe. There can be something a little frantic in her delivery, as though she has a list of a hundred items before her and what she's talking about now is only the tenth. Obviously she must get on. Experience has taught her to be a bit severe, and that's also her taste in clothes.

CHARLOTTE WOLF: The overworked librarian of this overcrowded high school feels she is fighting a losing battle to protect her library. The result is that she sometimes loses sight of the reason for having a library. She loves books so much she hates to see them get away into the hands of probably careless students--which makes it a little hard on the students. However, she is preserving her library. Often her speeches are in two parts--an invitation "This is your library" and then some version of "but you can't use it." Possibly she can use different tones for these two aspects of her announcements. She dresses conservatively.

SAMUEL BESTER: He is a brilliant English teacher who has had the misfortune of being made an administrator. However, he knows teaching and

89

teachers well, and his perceptive comments to Sylvia after observing her class are immediately upsetting to her but still genuinely helpful. His clothes may be just a trifle old-fashioned, but don't overdo this.

ELLA FRIEDENBERG: She is Guidance Counselor, and she takes her position quite seriously. (Some suspect, not without reason, that Ella fancies herself as a logical modern development of Sigmund Freud!) She constantly makes capsule characterizations of the students, cloaking these in psychiatric terms. She should speak this terminology correctly and with great authority. She wears her hair pulled back, and her clothes, to use her words, are aggressively plain.

FRANCES EGAN: She is the School Nurse, and she's an extremely interesting person. On the surface, and at first, she seems a bit of a "health nut" talking about nutrition and the importance of a hot breakfast. Actually, she's a woman who cares very much about the students but is utterly frustrated by the strict regulations that limit her ability to help. Her self-revealing speech in the last act should be delivered with unexpected force. She wears a white smock over her dress.

DR. MAXWELL CLARKE: He is the school principal but somehow separated from the immediate wear and tear of relationships to which the others are subjected. He likes to remain above the battle, and he does this by dealing in general terms. He has a mannerism of pairing words--aims and goals, healthful and fruitful, and so forth. He is impeccably dressed in a conservative business suit.

ELLEN: Not of the faculty, but another adult, Ellen is Sylvia's best friend "back home," a girl with whom Sylvia went through college. Ellen is concerned about Sylvia, and through their letters-- which often turn into direct conversation--they are quite close to each other. Ellen, like Sylvia, has an excellent sense of the humorous, and she is also rather wise. She wears attractive around-the-house clothes.

STUDENTS

JOE FERONE: He's a hostile, handsome young man with a high I.Q. but failing in almost every subject. He's been hit hard by the world outside, so hard that he protects himself against future disappointment by expecting the worst from every situation. What is really going on inside him, however, is revealed when he pauses before walking out of Sylvia's class and says "Too bad I can't believe you." He's a strong person, so much so that in the moment of self-revelation late in the play when he says "I'm tired of going up the down staircase," it carries a special force.

ALICE BLAKE: She's a romantic, whose reading is a mixture of some of the great literature about love along with some of the worst screen and television soap opera. She's a sensitive person, but too credulous and emotional to protect herself.

LINDA ROSEN: Quite different from Alice Blake, Linda is wise, attractive, and popular. Her whole focus, however, is in the opposite sex, and she hasn't the slightest interest in school except for its social utility. She dresses in a brighter and more feminine fashion than do the other girls.

HARRY A. KAGAN: He's the school politician and he works at it all the time. Actually, Harry, isn't quite as ingratiating or as successful in impressing others as he thinks, but his energy is tremendous. The actor playing this role should play it as though running for re-election. Harry dresses a bit better than the other boys.

HELEN ARBUZZI: Her role has the special value of being both the beginning and the end of the

91

play. By dropping out at the start of the play she represents the first defeat for Sylvia, and by coming back to school at the end, she represents a real reason for Sylvia to rejoice. There is nothing hostile in Helen's manner at the beginning of the play, she is simply dealing with what she feels to be "the facts of life." In the last act she should come on unobtrusively with the other students, and emerge as a surprise.

KATHERINE and FRAN: They are both office helpers, and while they remain students, their attitudes are a bit closer to those of the faculty. Like Sadie Finch they should give the appearance of having many, many things to do and very little time in which to cover them all. As they are often messengers for Mr. McHabe and Sadie, they often-- unconsciously--assume some of their authority. Katherine is the more impatient messenger, while Fran is usually bored-out-of-her-mind.

CHARLES ARRONS: While he likes to "horse around," he also has a sensitivity to good writing as he reveals in one of his comments from the suggestion box.

CARRIE BLAINE: She's an outspoken girl and always ready to give anyone her frank opinion. In addition to her school work she has to work very hard at home and this may give an added edge to her comments.

ELIZABETH ELLIS: She has genuine literary ability, but she's at a time in life when she takes herself with great seriousness, and her writing even more so. That will probably change later, but right now her over-serious dramatic presentations of her own writing is often humorous. Her seriousness about her studies, however, serves another important function in the play by providing a contrast in attitudes to other students.

RUSTY O'BRIEN: He is going through an anti-girl phase which makes it difficult for him because he likes Sylvia so well. He is quite sensitive to the relationships between the other students and is aware, for example, of Sylvia's desire to salvage what hope she can for the rebellious Joe Ferone.

RACHEL GORDON: She's an attractive girl, and there's a little undercurrent of feeling in her for Lou Martin, though its only actual expression is in a protest against his showing off which she speaks as one of her "suggestions." When possible, however, she reacts, through her expressions, to Lou's antics--usually with disgust. But at the end, when Lou rejoins the class, she's delighted.

LOU MARTIN: He's the class comedian. When he says he has to go for a drink of water, obviously he's about to die from thirst. Actually, he's a bit insecure, and his "ha ha" is spoken to cover this--such as in his reference to his father's comment that when Lou turns seventeen, he'll be just another mouth to feed, adding "Ha, ha--that's me." When Lou comes back to class at the end, his manner should suggest that he has not only won some off-stage battle with his family, but also with himself.

LENNIE NEUMARK: He's close to Lou, and they enjoy each other, though Lennie is a bit tougher. Words come easily to Lennie, and he enjoys throwing them around just as he enjoys his mock indignation or whatever he's putting on right now.

JILL NORRIS: She's another attractive girl and one involved in many activities--such as the high school paper. She's a bright girl and she'd like the opportunity to show this off. She'll probably do quite well in the future.

EDWARD WILLIAMS: He is black, sometimes sullen and suspicious, not without reason. He has encountered so much prejudice in the world outside that sometimes he suspects it where it doesn't really exist. When he insists on being called Edward Williams, Esquire, he is demanding respect not only for himself but for everyone black.

CAROLE BLANCA: She changed her name from Carmelita to Carole, and she loves her new name. She's an affectionate, warm-hearted girl, and because she used to sit close to Alice Blake she is involved with the trouble that comes to Alice.

JOSE RODRIGUEZ: He is a shy young man, and a very lonely one. It's typical of Jose to have the only recognition that will come on his birthday be a note to himself about it in the suggestion box, which he signs "Me." The scene in which Jose emerges from his shell encouraged by Sylvia, during the classroom discussion about Macbeth, should be played in definite stages by Jose--and in the end, having proven himself, he's a much more confident person.

VIVIAN PAINE: The underlying difficulty in her life, or so she feels, is that she thinks both her sister and Sylvia are much more attractive than she is. Her comment that she is only unhappy at home but never in Sylvia's class is also important to her character. There is a subtle shift in her toward greater self-confidence as the play progresses.

GENERAL NOTE: Costumes worn by the students should be typical school clothes. The only exception from the norm would be that Linda wears clothes a bit louder than the other girls', Harry Kagan wears more conservative clothes, Vivian shifts to more attractive clothes in the second act by which time she is liking herself better, and Ferone should wear dark clothes so he stands out from the others--perhaps a black leather jacket.

PROPERTY LIST

GENERAL: Divider or wall section with door, teacher's desk and chair, blackboard with chalk and eraser, twelve desk-chairs or small chairs with desks, platform with cut-outs (see description on page 6 and diagram on page 146). For Act Two: "Suggestion Box" printed on cut-outs at L and R ends. English lesson, including diagramed sentence, written on blackboard and a note to pick up a sup-plementary reading list from Miss Barrett's desk, and a message that reads "Miss B. I'm here so don't count me absent. The reason I'm not here is because I'm in the office. Carole."

SYLVIA: Attendance cards, roll book, a number of papers of various colors and sizes, test book-lets, papers, pen, etc.

DR. MAXWELL CLARKE: Hand microphone (optional).

ALICE BLAKE: Papers (homework).

ELIZABETH ELLIS: Paper (Act Two).

FRANCINE GARDNER: Slip of paper, another piece of paper; two papers (memo-announcement), blank form.

HELEN ARBUZZI: Slip of green paper.

CHARLES ARRONS: Slip of green paper (Act Two).

EDWARD WILLIAMS: Paper.

KATHERINE WOLZOW: Paper (blank form) and paper (announcement); papers.

PAUL BARRINGER: Board eraser, watch (Act One). Sheet of paper with writing on it (Act Two).

JOE FERONE: Slip of paper (Act One). Book report (Act Two).

CHARLOTTE WOLF: Slip of paper.

ELLEN: Opened letter.
ALL STUDENTS: Books, notebooks, pencils, etc.

WHAT PEOPLE ARE SAYING about *Up the Down Staircase*...

"Perfectly suited for a high school play. It's a great way to get a lot of people involved. The set is designed for the student to add his/her creative additions!"   *Scott McDonald,*
Chenango Forks High School, Binghamton, N.Y.

"*Up the Down Staircase* is a timeless representation of issues surrounding teenagers. The fast single-line dialogue is energizing."   *Lana Jean Baker,*
Plano High School, Plano, Ill.

"Awesom play to do for first-time or inexperienced directors. Easy to cast and publicize as it offers a great representation of the educational culture."   *Robbin Demeester,*
Rockford High School, Rockford, Mich.

"A great opportunity for 'ensemble' cast work. Relevant, fun and well suited to high school actors/audiences."   *Keith Malcolm,*
F.W. Johnson Collegiate H.S., Regina, SK

"The play worked perfectly—students acting like students! The set was a challenge, but we were VERY proud of our version. The cast was a great size for variety but also gave us a sense of camaraderie."   *J. Wainwright,*
Northland Pines High School, Green Bay, Wis.

"Enjoyable production for the director due to variety of characters and scenes. Great for high school kids because they can relate to the characters. Teachers who saw our production said it reminded them of their first year of teaching! Very fun play. Nice community event."   *Chris Rees,*
Chugiak High School, Eagle River, Alaska